NOVELS BY **BURT WEISSBOURD**

Callie and Cash Thrillers

Danger in Plain Sight

Rough Justice

Out of the Past

Corey Logan Thrillers

Inside Passage

Teaser

Minos

In Velvet

(a thriller set in Yellowstone National Park)

Danger in Plain Sight

"Here's what happens when you enter Mr. Weissbourd's world: You can't get out. You will be astonished not only by the colorful, playful, lethal characters, you will be hooked into a plot that laughs at whatever else you thought you were doing today. Callie and Cash, beauty and the beast, and the characters that swim through their world are each a gem of humanity observed."

—**David Field**, screenwriter and former head of West Coast Production United Artists

"Weissbourd delivers a polished page-turner about terrorism, money laundering, and the price of sins rooted in avarice."

—BlueInk Review

"From the author of the brilliant Corey Logan Trilogy, *Danger in Plain Sight* is the latest thriller from Burt Weissbourd and his finest novel yet. Weissbourd has created an entire genre—*Seattle Noir*. Callie James and her son, Lew, are indelible characters. I devoured the novel in a single night–and I think you will, too."

—**Jacob Epstein**, writer and executive story editor *Hill Street Blues*, writer *LA Law*

"A woman gets in touch with her inner action hero in this bracing thriller."

—Kirkus Reviews

Inside Passage

"A narrative that is relentlessly taut and exciting."

—***Foreword Reviews***

"*Inside Passage* hit all the hallmarks of a great read… Riveting story from the first paragraph."

—***Nightly Reading***

"The family dynamics and insights to human behavior had me reeling…. Juicy, fascinating stuff."

—***The (Not Always) Lazy W***

"*Inside Passage* is a great thriller and the restaurants you include as part of the story: Canlis, El Gaucho, Tulio, Queen City Grill, Wild Ginger, are all very sexy places. You really captured our city!"

—**Scott Carsburg**, James Beard award winner
and legendary Seattle chef

"I got completely hooked on *Inside Passage*""

—**Nancy Guppy**, host of *Art Zone* on Seattle Channel

Teaser

"A stunning, fast-paced thriller."

—***Roxy's Reviews***

"Burt Weissbourd is such a great writer... Such a great book!"

—***So I Am a Reader***

"Weissbourd, a seasoned screenwriter and film producer, has the mechanics down pat. Teaser is a fun, action-filled ride."

—***Foreword Reviews***

"Weissbourd's stellar writing, memorable characters and an extremely well-crafted narrative never disappoint."

—***Discerning Reader***

Minos

"Original, consistently compelling...Minos is an exceptionally entertaining and engaging read from beginning to end."

—***Midwest Book Review***

"These books transcend the expectations of genre fiction to become literature."

—**Jacob Epstein**, writer and executive story editor of *Hill Street Blues*, writer *LA Law*

"Mr. Weissbourd draws you into a world of characters and stories that keep you riveted, and you're pretty sure you are visiting people and worlds that have little or nothing to do with you. But he keeps going deeper, and by the end, he has delivered you back to yourself, a self you may not have admitted to before. Mr. Weissbourd, please keep writing."

—**David Field**, screenwriter and former head of West Coast Production United Artists

In Velvet

"This thrilling novel has a breathless pace that combines science and nature to create nail-biting tension."

—***Foreword Reviews***

"*In Velvet* left me breathless, a bit contemplative, and completely satisfied."

—***Manic Readers***

"Weissbourd's writing reminds me of the great Raymond Chandler mysteries."

—**John McCaffrey**, *KGB Bar Lit Mag*

"*In Velvet* is a thrill from start to finish!"

—***Closed the Cover***

HOPE DIES LAST

Out of the Past

"*Out of the Past* by Burt Weissbourd is wonderfully written with various twists and turns in a flawless plotline that kept me looking forward to subsequent chapters... The steady narration was also excellent and added to the overall beauty of the book..."

—**Frank Mutuma,** ***Readers' Favorite***

"Abe Stein, the unique character in *Out of the Past*, is a most unlikely psychiatrist... But, he's a credible literary psychiatrist and very appealing... He is so good that I don't really know why the book is about Cash and moreover, I don't care. Just leave Abe alone. By and large, leave the book alone."

—**Arlene Heyman, MD**, (psychiatrist/psychoanalyst), author of Scary Old Sex and Artifact

"When he (Cash) and the therapist begin to explore his life for clues, the horrors from his past suddenly come alive as a real-life nightmare that puts him and his loved ones in grave danger. That's the fascinating premise of Out of the Past, the third book in Burt Weissbourd's Callie and Cash series—a twisty, fast-moving thriller that provides one shocking surprise after another ... if you're looking for some thrills and entertainment and fast-moving action, you can't go wrong with this book."

—**R. G. Belsky,** ***BookTrib***

BURT WEISSBOURD

HOPE DIES LAST

A CALLIE AND CASH THRILLER

BLUE CITY PRESS
ISLIP, NY

RARE BIRD
LOS ANGELES, CALIF.

THIS IS A GENUINE RARE BIRD | BLUE CITY PRESS BOOK

Rare Bird Books
6044 North Figueroa Street
Los Angeles, CA 90042
rarebirdbooks.com

Blue City Press
62 West Bayberry Road
Islip, NY 11751

TRADE PAPERBACK ORIGINAL EDITION

Jacket design by Lisa Fyfe

Printed in the United States

10 9 8 7 6 5 4 3 2 1

Publisher's Cataloging-in-Publication Data available upon request.

For my children and their spouses:
Ben and Pamela, Emily and Meghan, Jenny and Mariele

PROLOGUE

Sara and Alvaro were sitting side by side, alone, at his handsome, mahogany bar, a popular spot in his well-liked South Beach club, the Midnight Mirage. On Mondays, when the club was closed, they often gathered there, and tonight, they were sipping mojitos while he was on the phone. Sara was going over a memo - questions and notes from their accountant. When Alvaro finally hung up, finished, Sara looked up at him, waited for him to say something. When he didn't, she eventually asked, vaguely irritated, "So?"

"Sorry, hon, I'm still reeling. That was my cousin, Luis."

"No… Luis, the guy I met at our wedding?"

"Yes."

"I remember him, I liked him…" She hesitated, smiling, gently touching her husband's hand. "My God, that's been almost four years."

He kissed her, a tender, loving kiss, then, before she could ask, "He just got off a plane. He was in a taxi, and he wants to come here to see me…right now… He's close."

"Now? Out of nowhere… Why?"

"He didn't say anything except that it was important."

"Isn't he a journalist?"

"Yes. He's a sought after freelance foreign correspondent. He's coming now from Venezuela."

"Is this about a story?"

"He said he'd explain why when he saw me tonight, soon."

"Are you excited?"

"Very, he's as close as I have to an older brother…"

"Tell me more about that… You rarely see him. You don't even talk to me about him."

"It's a special kind of connection. He looked after me when I first came to Miami. I still call him when I want advice—"

The doorbell interrupted them. Alvaro quickly stepped down from the bar stool and moved to open the door. A tall man in a good-looking blue suit hugged him enthusiastically.

Sara watched, pleased that Alvaro seemed so happy.

Luis stepped back, then kissed his cousin on both cheeks. Alvaro hugged him again, then led him to the bar where Luis gracefully kissed Sara's hand, then embraced her warmly. He stepped back. "Wonderful to see you again, Sara. You're even more beautiful than I remember."

"Thank you, Luis." She bowed, just slightly. "You're every bit as charming as I remember, and you're getting almost as good looking as my stunning Cuban husband."

"I'm flattered," Luis nodded. "Though I'm not sure I accept the 'almost.'"

Alvaro smiled warmly, behind the bar, making his cousin a mojito. He added two teaspoons of honey. He passed it to his cousin, motioning for him to sit on the bar.

His cousin sat, raised his glass, a toast, "To Sara and Alvaro. I'm simply thrilled to be with you."

They all touched glasses then took a sip.

"Did I get your mojito right?" Alvaro asked his cousin.

"Perfect," Luis replied. "I'm sure you want to know why I'm here so suddenly, so let me explain now, and then we can arrange a time to catch up and celebrate."

"Please," Alvaro said.

"I'm on a very big story. You may have heard that about five years ago three hundred and fifty million dollars went missing from a Venezuelan military account in a state-owned oil company. The money was stolen, gone without a trace. For five years, no one has been able to find it. The Venezuelan mastermind, who was behind this, died soon after the money disappeared. I've been on the story for over three months. So far, I've gotten nothing significant, not even a plausible theory… just a few unlikely hunches. I know that Miami was, and is, a destination for laundering dirty Latin American money. I have a person here in Miami who's been looking around for me. My father recommended this young man. We chose him because he's been working in the office of a Miami international lawyer, Alberto Leon, who, in the past, often moved fair amounts of foreign money. So far, there's been no evidence of any illegal money transfers or money laundering. Leon's name came up coincidentally in my poking around in Venezuela. Nothing specific about him, but he seemed a starting place to learn more about moving money. Many of his clients use a bank in the Cayman Islands. Last week, my observer took a picture of this lawyer meeting in Miami with an unknown client, an American citizen born in Venezuela. He believes this former Venezuelan is a big shot, based on what the lawyer said about him, and how he said it. My guy gave me that photo, on a flash drive, just now at the airport. He's worried. The Venezuelan had two high powered security guys. The bodyguards have been keeping an eye on him. He gave them the slip before he went to the airport. My informant made me promise to protect the photo at all costs and to keep him out of it, period. I took a look right away. I recognized the lawyer. I didn't know the other man. I called a good Miami police officer, a detective, right away. I know and trust this man, and he's meeting with me first thing tomorrow morning. He's smart and he'll help. The reason I'm here now is because I need to protect this photo tonight. The banks are closed, so I was hoping you'd hide it, safely. I'll pick it up early this morning, on my way to the police. Can you do that?" He set the flash drive on the bar.

Alvaro took it, put it in his pocket. "Of course… Are you worried?"

"Not yet. But I've learned to be extra careful. I don't want to even know where you hid the photo."

"I'll take care of that."

"Thank you, my friend…" He paused to take a pen and a small notebook out of his jacket pocket. He wrote a name and a phone number on a small piece of paper. "Another extra precaution." He handed it to Alvaro. "This is the name and phone number of my friend, Rafael, the police detective. Call him whenever, you don't need a reason… Now, I should go. I'm very tired, and I want to call my dad."

"Can I get you a cab?"

"That would be helpful. My hotel is not too far… It's truly a pleasure to see both of you again."

"That pleasure is mutual." Sara embraced Luis. "I'd like to invite you to our house for dinner tomorrow night, give us that chance to catch up, to celebrate. I'll cook paella, Cuban style, if you'd like."

"Cuban paella! That would be a treat for me."

"Okay then. Let's say 7:00 p.m. You'll meet our son, and I'll include your father if you'd like."

"Perfect. I'd love to meet your son… I promised to see my dad tomorrow, but he'll be working all day, so dinner is ideal. I'll tell him later, when I call."

Alvaro smiled, then turned to his wife. "Sara, as always, you're ahead of me. This dinner is a very good idea. Well done."

Sara took his hand. "I'm lucky about your family. This is easy."

"No, sweetheart, you just made it seem easy," Alvaro nodded, certain.

Sara touched Alvaro's shoulder. "I have some paperwork to finish up here. Why don't you relieve the babysitter and put Young Cash to bed?"

"My pleasure, I'll see you at home… Luis, let's get that taxi." Alvaro shook his cousin's hand with both of his own, then he put his arm on Luis' shoulder and led him out the door.

CHAPTER ONE

It was almost 10:00 p.m., Alvaro was checking on Young Cash, who was asleep in his room. Alvaro pulled up his soft blue wool blanket until it covered his shoulders, kissed him gently, then returned to their living room. He thought about his young son, Y.C., and it brought a smile to his face. They'd started calling him Y.C. because it was simpler than Young Cash and less confusing than just Cash when his grandfather was around. Alvaro sat on his favorite Cuban lounge chair. It had a clean smooth profile with handwoven cotton straps. This iconic piece was a blend of comfort and talented Cuban craftsmanship. He looked around, enjoying the thoughtfully organized room, and tried to relax.

The living room was warm and colorful like their Art Deco South Beach house. It's vibrant pastel colors, geometric shapes and smooth streamlined forms were unique, stylish and tasteful, like them. The lovely room was filled with Cuban memorabilia—photos, mostly of Sara, taken from some of their favorite spots: Havana bars and restaurants; on a trip to one of the Caribbean's largest forest and one of the world's most preserved wetlands—near Cienaga de Zapata, a haven for wondrous birds, rare species of fish and animals; many of their preferred walking and shopping streets; a magnificent shot of Alvaro leading Sara salsa dancing - Sara twirling through the air. He smiled, glancing at contemporary artwork, at souvenirs they'd brought back including a hand-woven Cuban jute rug under a hand crafted Cuban two-tier mahogany coffee table, and so on.

Alvaro picked up the phone, dialing Sara at his club, again. No answer. Odd. He called Luis. He, too, didn't answer the phone. He tried calling the bar directly, no answer. Was she walking home? Unlike her to leave without calling him. He checked his watch, 10:15 p.m. He'd arrived home at 8:30 p.m. This was too long. Worried now, he picked Young Cash, still asleep, still wrapped in his blue blanket, out of his bed. He carried him outside, then set him down in his car seat in the back of the car. His club wasn't far, and less than ten minutes later they were there. He picked Young Cash out of his car seat. Y.C. was crying now, awake and confused. Alvaro hurried to the door which was unlocked. He opened the door to see the club totally trashed, ransacked – everything pulled out onto the floor. He couldn't see Sara. The long mahogany bar dominated the back of the room. Normally there were twenty tables placed neatly in front of the bar. Now they were sprawled haphazardly around the floor. Facing the bar, the office was off to the right in a small room. Still carrying a crying Young Cash, Alvaro hurried to open the office door. He cried out when he saw Sara. She was lying on the floor, tied up, struggling to breathe through her nose. Her head, face and arms were badly bruised and bloody. There were two open cuts, still bleeding, stubbornly, on the top of her head. Her mouth had been taped shut. There were tears on her cheeks. Alvaro set Y.C. down on the floor. He was looking at his mother, touching her arms and crying.

Alvaro gently removed the tape, then he untied her hands and feet. He hurried to the bathroom and came back with a wet towel that he carefully set on her head. During this, he asked, worriedly, "How badly are you hurt?"

"I'll live." She paused, took a slow painful breath.

"Can you tell me what you remember?"

Sara nodded, winced, took another breath. "There were two of them, skilled professionals… I got the first one, but I had to turn around… the other one cracked my head from behind, with some kind of billy club… twice…" She took another slow breath.

Alvaro frowned, took her hand.

"Sorry… let me catch my breath…"

"Take your time."

"…he knocked me out. I'll need a doctor for that…"

He looked again. "Yes."

She squeezed his hand. "Later, when I was tied up, they beat me up… my body, my arms, my face. They used the billy club again. I think they cracked one or two bones in my ribs…"

"Bastards… Were they after the photo?"

"Yes. They wanted to know where the flash drive was. I finally told them how to open the safe, since I was afraid they might kill me. I didn't know that you hadn't remembered to put the flash drive in there before you left."

"I'm sorry. I just forgot about it."

"Right… I did get that…" She nodded, made a wry face, painfully. "After that, they left me alone… Killing me wasn't their agenda… I heard them making noise. They spoke Spanish to each other. I'm guessing that they were opening files, checking every possible hiding place before they left."

"Yes. They trashed the entire club."

He helped her sit. Then, as Sara held her son in her arms, Alvaro brought her a cup of water. While she took a drink of water, he looked at the open safe. He checked his pant pocket - the flash drive was there. He held it up, showing it to Sara. "It was in my pocket."

Sara winced again, groaning, "…that's my guy …even when you screw up, you end up looking smart."

"Still got your special sense of humor." Alvaro smiled. "Good. I'm going to take you to the hospital right away. We'll take Y.C." He helped her up. She had trouble keeping her balance and Alvaro put his arm around her waist. She held Young Cash, who was doing better. In the car, he drove way too fast to the emergency room.

****

Alvaro held Y.C., and stayed with Sara until a doctor came in to examine her. He was young, maybe thirty, but he was smart, and he knew that Sara needed help right away. He prepped her for stitches, and gave her two shots for pain. Once Alvaro was convinced that she was in good hands, he stepped outside with Y.C. He pulled a chair next to her room, sat the baby on his lap, then called Luis. No answer. Next, he called Cash. Cash was eating upstairs, at their table in the corner of the bar in Callie's restaurant.

Alvaro jumped right in. "Sara's OK, but she's been beaten up… Please, just listen. We're at the hospital. She'll have stitches where she was cracked on the head, but she should be home tomorrow… She was attacked in my bar. It's not about us, but they're after something we have… It's a backup photo stick, a flash drive, that my cousin Luis gave to me, and asked me to hide… In the photo, there's a lawyer and someone else we don't recognize… I think there's still danger… Yes, I think you should come right away… I'll call you later, as soon as she's resting, and tell you everything I know… Yes, bring Callie. Sara will like that, not to mention Young Cash…. Thank you." Alvaro hung up.

He stood up, walking Y.C. now as he made a second call. "Detective, I'm Luis's cousin. I can't find him. He said to call you if I needed help… My wife was badly beaten in our bar soon after he left… They wanted the flash drive with the photo… It wasn't there… I'm worried about Luis… He was going to his hotel, I'd also check his father… We're at the hospital… I'll see you there."

Alvaro made one more call, to their friend, Maria. She was Cuban and had worked for years at his bar.

He spoke Spanish. "Maria, it's Alvaro. I'm sorry to wake you, but we need your help. Sara was beaten up at the bar. She'll be okay. We're at the hospital, the one nearby… Y.C. is confused and upset about what happened to his mom. Can you come and take care of her?... Just stay with him at the hospital to begin. I need to talk with Sara, the police and others… You're a treasure."

****

Alvaro was sleeping in a chair in Sara's room. She, too, was sound asleep in the hospital bed they'd assigned to her. It was 2:30 a.m. A knock on the door woke Alvaro up. He opened the door to an older well-worn policeman with two other policemen behind him.

"Hello," the policeman began. "I'm Detective Rafael, Luis's friend." He showed Alvaro his ID, then said. "You must be Alvaro. We talked on the phone…"

"Yes, of course."

"I'm sorry to show up like this, but I wanted to talk to you now, in person."

Alvaro nodded, concerned about Rafael's expression.

Rafael pointed at the other policemen behind him. "These men work for me and they're here to protect you and your family."

Alvaro looked at all of them. "Why?"

"I'm sorry, but—"

"What's wrong?" just came out of Alvaro's mouth.

"After you called, I went looking for Luis. When I couldn't reach him on the phone, I called his father, Miguel." He paused, clearly upset. "He hadn't heard from him yet. He came with me to his hotel. I'm sorry to tell you this… but we found him dead in his room."

"No, oh no…" Alvaro cried out, "Oh, Jesus, no…" He covered his eyes, tearing now. "How...?"

"He was beaten, then they slit his throat."

"His father saw him like that?"

"Yes. He was beside himself. He stayed there, and I rushed here. Is there anyone at your house?"

"No, I took the baby and came to find my wife."

"I'm sure that these killers are after the photo that Luis gave to you. And I'd bet that they're looking for you now. I sent several policemen to check your house. I should hear from them soon… Now, I'd like to see the photo."

Alvaro thought about this, then he decided to tell him the truth, "Not yet, I need to talk with someone first. His name is Cash, and he's in charge."

"I'm a police officer, and I need to see the photo."

"Please don't make this difficult, officer. Just give me time to talk with him."

"When can you talk to him?"

"He's on his way here from Seattle. I'll have an answer as soon as he calls this morning."

"I'll give you tell then, this morning, max."

"Thank you."

"What's in this photo?"

"There's a lawyer, someone Luis recognized, and someone else we couldn't identify. He's wearing a high-tech, covid mask, and it hides his face."

"Who's the lawyer?"

"Luis said his name is Alberto Leon. Luis's father, Miguel, knows him. He's Venezuelan. That's all I know."

Rafael's phone rang. He listened, then he said, "Okay. Stay there, and I'll get back to you." He closed his phone, turned to Alvaro. "They broke into your house. They searched everywhere. They turned it upside down. Did you hide it there?"

"No."

"Then they're looking for you now. Probably on their way here already. I know a temporary safe house where we can hide you and your family. We should go there right away." He looked at Alvaro, who was distracted. "That means right this minute."

"Okay. I'm on it." He went over to wake Sara.

He considered giving Rafael a copy of the photo, but he decided against it. Alvaro knew, somehow, that he had to talk with Cash before he turned this photo over to the police.

"Rafael and one of the other policemen already had Sara in a cot, and they were wheeling her, hurrying her out the door and down the hall.

Alvaro followed, calling Maria as he moved. "Bring Y.C. to his car seat right away. We're leaving now. Hurry."

When they got to the parking lot Alvaro pointed out their car.

Rafael took charge. "I'll drive you, your wife and your boy. My man will drive the babysitter home."

In no time, they had Sara in the back with Y.C., Alvaro sat up front with Rafael, then they were gone.

****

Two fit, well-dressed, Venezuelan men, Carlos and Ruben, were sitting in the spacious aft deck eating area on Stanley White's 115' 6" Sunseeker 116 yacht. The yacht was anchored in a protected island cove, within easy striking distance to Miami. It was 7:30 a.m. and they were drinking coffee. Their boss, Stanley White, the man in the photo, was staring at them across a crafted wooden table, under a covered eating area. Even though he was wearing a covid mask, they could see how angry he was. They could see the rage in his bright blue eyes.

"No photo, no idea where it is, no idea where they are?... I'm dumbfounded... speechless... You were specially chosen years ago, trained extensively, generously paid... I trusted you... Are you stupid? No! Were you unprepared for unexpected risks? No! Were you poorly trained? No!... How in hell could we find ourselves here?"

Carlos, the oldest, well-dressed in an expensive suit, replied, politely, "Sir, we will find them. We will take the flash drive, then they will disappear."

White responded, plainly annoyed, "They've disappeared already... You don't know how to find them. Not a clue... and the photo may have been circulated."

Carlos' face fell, "Sir, I believe, in fact, I'm confident–"

"Enough... First, never, ever talk to me in that simplistic, glib tone... furthermore, before you say another word, think precisely, carefully, about what you are saying, about what it means... Am I clear?" then ice cold, "Crystal clear?"

Carlos took a look in his eyes. "My apologies. Sir, it won't happen again."

"I hope not... Remember, we don't know how many others have seen the photo. What we do know is the potential consequences to us if anyone becomes curious about the man talking with Counselor Alberto Leon…"

Ruben, an experienced middle-aged killer, with a hard, rugged face, stood, "Respectfully, that's unlikely sir. We have been extremely careful… there's no interest in you… You're invisible…"

"We're at risk, gentlemen…" Stanley White sighed, nodding, he knew that was true. He went on, forcefully, "And lest we forget, you've endangered our invisibility… You've killed the employee of the lawyer I'm trusting. You've killed a well-known journalist. You've badly beaten a young woman who knows nothing. And now, you propose to kill all of the others who might know, whoever they might be... Remember, everyone you hurt or kill potentially attracts attention to us. And for us to remain unnoticed, you know we don't want attention."

Ruben spoke softly but forcibly, "We're sorry, sir, but please, don't underestimate us. We can and will eliminate them, discretely, whatever it takes. We will remain anonymous. It's what we know how to do."

"How can you do that when you can't find them?"

Ruben replied patiently, "Please just hear me out, sir… We need your help to find them. Talk with your lawyer friend. He'll have a police contact, someone on the inside. We went to the hospital. They'd already left, but a nurse told us that there were three policemen who left with them. You find out your lawyer's police contact. Have your lawyer ask him where they went. We'll take it from there."

Mr. White took a slow breath then said, "Okay, that may be helpful… Just remember, never forget, that there are consequences if you don't succeed. Our adversaries were, and still are, humiliated… and they're enraged. At their best, they're ruthless and unforgiving. Now, at their worst?... For your sake, for all of us, you don't want to be wrong."

****

The little condo that Rafael put them in was nondescript in a lower middle-class area in the interior of South Beach. It was facing a parking lot and there was an old shopping street with several restaurants around the corner. In the living room, Sara, Alvaro and Rafael had brought Cash up to date. Then, Alvaro had taken Cash out to the old, enclosed patio, where he showed him the photo in the flash drive.

Cash took his computer out from a bag he carried out with him, then set it on an open wooden picnic table. He sat on the wooden bench, then Cash stuck the flash drive into the appropriate slot in his laptop. Next, he downloaded the photo. Finally, he emailed one copy to Andre, another to the Macher, Cash's Yiddish nickname for Itzac, his old, trusted friend. When he was finished, he called each of them, connecting them to a conference call on his cell phone. He quickly explained how the photo was given to Luis and how he passed it on to Alvaro. He then detailed the break in at Alvaro's bar, the attack on Sara, then the subsequent break in at their home, and finally killing Luis at the hotel. He explained that they were safe now, hidden by Rafael, Luis's policeman friend, in a nondescript, empty house. What they needed now was their help to identify the masked man in the photo.

"Do you know the other man in the photo?"

"Luis knew the man without the mask," Cash answered. "He told us his name was Alberto Leon, and that he was a little-known Venezuelan lawyer in Miami."

"Tell us more about Luis," the Macher asked.

Alvaro answered, "Luis, my cousin, was an international journalist. He was trying to write an article about that three hundred and fifty million that went missing from the Venezuelan military about five years ago. The lawyer, Alberto Leon, often moved money from Venezuela, though his methods were generally through a Cayman Island bank and known to be legal. He kept a low profile, stayed below the radar. Luis' father, Miguel, who's on his way here, is also a lawyer, though not on the same level, and he's done some work for Alberto."

The Macher added, "Yes, I heard about that stolen money. It disappeared from an oil company. It was a state-owned oil company and the military used it for discretely purchasing very expensive long-term equipment, hard to find materials and machinery, and large quantities of oil. The missing money was military money, so this was red hot. It was never recovered."

"Can you learn more?"

"Yes. I did a deal several years ago with a Venezuelan general who was trading in precious Venezuelan metals, largely gold and diamonds. He was trading legally through some of the state mines. He's smart, and though he no longer lives there, he's still connected, and at least with me, he was honest. I'll call him. He'll know more."

Andre jumped in. "Not long ago, I worked for a Venezuelan military colonel on a mercenary operation in Guyana. I'll see what I can learn. I can tell you already that you don't want to mess around with these guys. I'm fairly sure that you're already on their hit list. To put it more specifically, I'd say that you're about to be attacked, likely ravaged by lethal scorpions. For now, the best thing, the smartest thing you can do is just dive under freezing cold water and stay hidden until I get there… I'm on it, and I'll book the next flight to Miami."

"You have a gift with words, Andre," the Macher chuckled. "I'll be there today," he added.

"Thanks to both of you," Cash said. "I'm sorry about the occasion."

"Who else has seen this photo?" the Macher asked.

"Just Alvaro, Sara and us."

Alvaro added, "Rafael, the policeman wants to see it."

Cash spoke up. "Since you told me that, I've been thinking about it. Rafael seems like a good man, I'll talk to him when we're done about showing it to a limited specific group - local detective colleagues in homicide, financial and organized crime. I'll set it up so that he doesn't go any further without checking with me. Let's see what he comes up with."

"Keep the group small," the Macher agreed. "No one else should see it, no wider distribution, until we find out what we're dealing with."

Andre added, "And then, if we find out it's related to the missing three hundred and fifty million dollars—well, it's too late to give it back.

They're going to have to kill you… Keeping you alive is going to be a fulltime nightmare—"

Cash interrupted, "Andre, try not to make a bad thing worse."

"How could it get worse?"

"You could do that… but my dear old friend, let's deal with that when we know more… For now, I'll handle it with Rafael…and right away, let's talk with Miguel. Let's get his help with Alberto."

****

When Cash and Alvaro came back inside, Sara was lying down on the living room sofa. Her head was resting on Callie's lap and Callie was holding her hand. Y.C. was asleep in his crib. Rafael was in the corner, on the phone. Sara looked up at Cash and her husband sitting across the coffee table. "I have to say this… it's been on my mind, bothering me… I'm feeling pretty foolish, even stupid… I mean Dad, I'm the one that forced you to change your lifestyle, your work. I insisted that our family had to make substantive changes, then I participated, whole heartedly, in putting together our plan for a year on a boat, where we all worked hard to figure out how we could create a safe way of life for our whole family. Everyone struggled, and finally succeeded, to design a new way of life, and we've followed our plan. Dad, you haven't been working on risky deals with the Macher or Andre. You're not making dangerous trades. We're spending time together in safe places. You and Callie come to us every few months for a relaxed family visit. You, grandpa, stay on for at least a week to help us with the baby, who's come to adore you. We come two or three times a year to Seattle. We take trips together, like going to France last spring. It's actually been working out as we planned, it's even been fun, as I'd hoped. Then just when we were supposed to be safe, relaxed, just fine… The most dangerous thing yet came after Alvaro and me for no reason I can understand, except bad luck." Sara started to cry.

Cash stood, then sat down beside her, gently saying, "Sweetheart, I understand how you feel. Please remember that our plan is still excellent, but whatever we do, however we try, we can't legislate safety. And as much as you hated the danger it exposed to you and your family, I'm sure that today you still appreciate that our unconventional team, and all of the resources it has, will be here soon to help keep you and your family safe."

"Yes, that's true, but I'd hoped we were beyond this kind of horrific, life-threatening danger."

"We are beyond some of it, but even if you live locked up in a fortress with no friends or even visitors, you're vulnerable to life's unexpected dangers… you know that, we talked carefully about that possibility."

Sara started crying again.

Y.C. began crying in his crib. Alvaro was right there, picking him up and walking him around the room. When he was calm, Alvaro gracefully set him back down again in his crib. He gently massaged his neck, until he was sleeping again.

Sara, still crying, watched her family, then said, "I didn't want to fear for my young child's safety, for his life, again, and now, I'm worried and it's before his third birthday."

"Of course you didn't want that again, but it didn't work out, and now we all need to make sure that Baby Cash, and his mother and father are safe. It's the best we can do…"

Sara kept on crying, taking her dad's hand. "I'm sorry I'm so naïve, so Pollyanna-ish – I learned that word from you, by the way_"

Callie jumped in, "Sara, your dad's word, Pollyanna-ish, is sometimes okay, a hopeful way to be, and you are—well—you're just so very cool… In fact, it's a wonder you can still be Pollyanna-ish, with the life you've lived." She used a piece of Kleenex to wash away Sara's tears. "You're young, you have a wonderful husband, a lovely baby boy, and your whole life is ahead of you. Let's get past this moment of sadness, face the bad, troubling news, and move on."

"How did you get so fearless, so helpful when things are so bad?"

"Your dad taught me all of that. When I met him, I was afraid to do anything…"

"I've never seen that."

"Part of me still feels that, but I've learned to live differently. And truthfully, though I supported and still believe in our plan, though I know how important it is to avoid unnecessary, foolish risks, I'm pleased, even proud, to have some of you and your dad's ability to manage hard, dangerous things."

Sara took both of their hands. "So, in your gentle, nice way, you're both telling me to stop—well—stop whining… Just fucking man up…."

"Well, not exactly…" Callie added, "I mean I would never say 'Just fucking man up.'"

"In your way, you sort of did…"

"I did?"

"No matter. It's done, I'm in."

Cash suggested, "For now, just take care of yourself, get well. You're welcome to be more involved when you're ready."

"I'm ready, dad… I need to be in on this—for Christ's sake, they beat me up…" She put her head up.

Cash shook his head. "I should have known."

Callie laughed. "Honey, don't be so protective. She's every bit as good as you, and you're great together."

"Okay, okay… Sara, you're in."

Sara sat up. "Good."

Rafael, who'd been listening to this, came over. "Before we get going, please let me see the photo?"

Cash turned to him, "Okay, I'll give you a copy of the photo. You're a good man, and we appreciate your help, but before I do that, I'm going to set up some restrictions. Please only show this photo to trusted colleagues who have a reason to see it. By that I mean police officers who are at high levels enforcing areas that might have reason to deal with and therefore recognize this man. That is to say organized crime, homicide, and financial crimes. Start there, and then let's talk again if you want to go further."

"Who are you? You can't tell me who to show this photo to."

"If you want to see it, you'll play by my rules."

"We're going to have problems. Don't push me too far. And while we're setting up ground rules, I'll want to know more about the men you're working with—their backgrounds, their current work status, relevant history, and so on."

"These are trusted colleagues, old friends, and their backgrounds, current work status and history are private. I won't give out any further information about them."

Rafael glared at him, getting angry. "Don't be stupid. How can I help you if I don't know what's going on, who I'm working with? Who in the hell do you think you are? Do I need to arrest you?"

"Let's try again." Cash touched his shoulder. "You don't know me. Please call Sergeant Lincoln in the LA Police department or Detective Ed Samter in the Seattle PD. Ask them about me, then tell them that I'm holding back evidence, and specifically, holding back further information about Itzac, the Macher, and my friend Andre. Please also tell them that I said it's important. They'll explain. I anticipated this and wrote down their phone numbers for you." He handed the policeman a piece of paper.

Rafael scowled, red-faced now, then went back to the corner to make the calls.

Alvaro's phone rang. He listened then went to the door. He opened the door, then embraced Miguel, Luis's devastated dad.

****

Rafael was arguing into the phone, "Detective Samter, I don't care if he's experienced in these matters, he can't cut me out… What do you mean I can't stop him… Who is this guy?... He's the smartest, best guy at this kind of dangerous work that you've ever met…? Working with him, it's like being in a Tarantino movie… Pulp Fiction?... Yes, I know how unexpected things happen in that movie… Pretend I'm in that movie…? What the hell are you talking about? Cash is Samuel L. Jackson as Jules… his partner, Andre, who's coming, is like John Travolta…? With

Cash — nothing is like it's supposed to be—crazy, violent things happen out of nowhere, and important things often work out against all odds in unexpected ways…? Detective Samter, are you fucking crazy?... I don't care if you don't appreciate my language…. You know Jim Holden, my Captain…? No, please don't call him… Okay, I'll make this deal with you. I'll give Mr. Pulp Fiction three days to do things his way. I'll do this if, and only if, after those three days, you call my Captain and tell him what an outstanding, exceptionally helpful policeman I am… You would actually do that, happily, for Mr. Pulp Fiction?"

****

Miguel's eyes were red from crying. He took off his coat, lay it over a nearby chair, then set his briefcase beside it. Alvaro put his arm over his shoulder and introduced him to Sara, Cash, and Callie.

Soon after, Rafael, who he'd met earlier, joined them. Rafael took over and spoke to Cash, "Both of them vouched for you. Nothing about it was normal. The LA sergeant said—like this was normal—how I'd likely get a raise if I stuck with you. Is he lying?... No comment?... The Seattle guy talked about *Pulp Fiction*, no kidding… He compared you to Samuel L. Jackson…"

Callie interrupted, "He's way cooler than Samuel L. Jackson. You'll see."

"Jesus… All I see so far is that your husband attracts the outliers, the weirdos… Cash, you're already a first-class nut job in my book, but I'll back you up on your own terms for three days. This is totally out of character for me. Don't make me sorry."

"Thank you. I'll try not to disappoint—"

Alvaro interrupted, "He won't disappoint you... Truthfully Detective, we can sort out these concerns later. Now, we have more important work to do." Alvaro turned to Miguel, put his hand on Miguel's shoulder. "I'm sorry to do this now, but we need your help right away."

"What can I do?" Miguel asked.

"Tell us whatever you can about the lawyer, Alberto Leon."

"He's a successful lawyer. He keeps a low profile, and he's carved out his own specific niche. He helps people, mostly Venezuelans, bring money into this country. He does this legally, and he's never been convicted of money laundering."

"How does he manage that?" Cash asked.

"He's ultra conservative about it. He's been prosecuted several times in the past ten years, but there's never been a conviction. I've thought about this, and I think, and this is just my interpretation, he's very careful not to touch any money that isn't already clean."

"How does he do that?" Callie asked.

"Here's what I'm guessing. The money may have been illegally obtained, but before Alberto even considers it, it must be carefully disguised, smurfed, layered, removed from the country. By the time Alberto will touch it, it's origins must be untraceable. In other words, it's already been laundered. He's extremely careful about that. What he does is move clean money into the country."

"Why would anyone use him if they've already successfully laundered the money?" Callie asked.

"Suppose the client doesn't want anyone to know that he's brought money in, even if it's legal. Alberto safely disguises the owner. For example, he often uses an influential Cayman Islands bank to distribute well-laundered money to shell companies and then the true owners are invisible, but I reiterate, he'll only use shell companies legally."

Cash nodded. "I know about that. Once the origin of the money is untraceable, and likely it's already been moved around the globe, it's safe to use a shell company, and then it's impossible to know whose money it is."

Callie asked, "How do you know about Alberto?"

"I've done quite a few mid-level jobs for him over the years. For a little more than the last three years, he's sent me real estate buyers to several large real estate developments he's representing. I handle their contracts and help them negotiate their deal."

“Anything special about the buyers or the developments?” Rafael asked.

“The developments are first class, all top-rated. There are three of them that I know of, one each in Naples, Fort Myers and the Marco Island region. You may know of them, like Silver Lake or Hancock Ranch. All three locations are ranked as among the top ten fastest growing places in the US They’re all good houses in good safe neighborhoods. Prices range from three hundred to one point four million. The average home price in the Naples development is over eight hundred thousand. One day, there will be over 120 houses in each development. The ranch has over 1200 acres and is eventually planning on building three hundred homes. They’re all still growing. The buyers are from all over—New York, California, Chicago, Boston, Houston, New Orleans, you name it, and, of course, Florida.”

Cash did the math. “I’m guessing they’ve already committed over two hundred and fifty million. Someone is putting a lot of money into these developments.”

“Yes, though that’s where the shell companies often kick in. The investors are totally unknown.”

“Could the other man in the photo be related to these developments?” Sara asked, still lying down on the couch.

Miguel nodded. “It’s possible, though I don’t know. All I heard was that Alberto was meeting an important client.”

“The other man in the picture is wearing a surgical covid mask and apparently was traveling with bodyguards. Suppose he’s the client who was meeting with Alberto. Do you know anything about that meeting?” Alvaro asked.

“No, I knew the man who took the photo. I introduced him to my son. His name was Garcia. He was a young man who ran errands for Alberto’s secretary. I tried to reach him several times earlier, but I couldn’t. He’s never been so hard to reach, especially so early in the morning… I hate to say this, but if he took the photo, I’d bet that he was also murdered.”

Sara joined in, sitting now on the couch, "That's two murders. There's also two break ins and the attack on me. That's a lot of risk for one photo. It's way too much. I just don't get it… We need to identify the man with the mask, right away," she asserted, with her characteristic certainty.

Miguel volunteered, "Before the man came, I went to bring some buyer documents to Alberto's office. One of the women I work with told me Alberto was expecting an important visitor, a client he'd never met in person. That's all I know."

Alvaro offered. "This is just speculation, but suppose some – or all - of the developments are being financed through the missing Venezuelan military money? Maybe that's what Luis was after. No one would ever find it, even guess it was here. Maybe the masked man was the dead general's contact in the US Maybe he moves the clean money to Alberto, who invests it. That would be sufficient reason to start killing people."

Cash stood. "Whoa… Let's not go too fast. This could be huge, but we don't know that any of it is true. First, let's see what more we can learn… Miguel, can you get any of Luis's notes?"

"Yes, I have some of them, I took his briefcase from his apartment. I have it here."

"Callie, Sara and I will pour through his notes, right away. In the meantime, Miguel, can you help us learn more about Alberto?"

"Like what?"

"His other clients, his colleagues in his firm, his connections in Venezuela, his history. Andre and the Macher will help you. They'll both be here within hours."

"OK, I'll tell them whatever I can, and here is my son's briefcase." Miguel pointed it out, Alvaro passed it over to Cash.

Rafael had stepped away to take a phone call. He came back to the group, addressing Cash, "I just had a request from a senior police officer, a lieutenant. He wanted to know where he could find you. He said he had info about the break-ins. I told him I didn't know where you were."

"Good."

"I'm sure he didn't believe me."

"What will he do?"

"He won't quit."

"Do the other two policemen who were at the hospital know where we are?"

"No, I sent them back to the office, after returning the sitter."

"Smart. Can he find this house in some file?"

"No. It's off the books. It belongs to someone who often works with me. I sent him away on another job. He's out of the country for at least a week. I have permission to use his house, but no one knows I'm using it."

"What do you know about the officer who asked?"

"Not a lot. He's experienced, a big shot, name is Tom Franklin."

"Can you find out if he knows or has been in touch with the lawyer, Alberto Leon?"

"Wouldn't surprise me. He's political and well connected. If he's connected with him though, he won't tell me about it… Look, I can brace him, ask others around the station."

"Thanks."

After a beat, Rafael turned back to Cash. "What's next? Time is of the essence, and, for better or worse, you're in charge now."

"I see. Okay, then let's you and I talk about what I'm thinking. First, I want to tell you what I can comfortably say about my friends, who will be here soon. They're unconventional and very capable. I think they can help us jump-start this."

"How?"

"That's what I need to talk with you about."

"More *Pulp Fiction*?"

"Better. Way better… these two guys coined 'relentless'… they're unstoppable. Buckle up, you're about to get help from the shark in *Jaws*… and the *Alien*."

CHAPTER TWO

Stanley White was sitting on a comfortable outdoor wooden cushioned chair facing a table on Alberto Leon's patio. They'd just sat down to eat a lavish lunch. It included a variety of seafood – king crab legs, shrimp, scallops, and lobster. There was an assortment of dipping sauces. There was fine white wine, white anchovy and crisp pita bread salad, an exotic side dish of Spanish wild rice, and more. Stanley complimented him on the excellent lunch, which he looked over slowly, carefully.

Alberto was sitting down with his private, secretive client for the very first time, and he knew that it was essential for him to re-establish an excellent, comfortable, working relationship. The unexpected, potentially dangerous photo had created considerable tension, and he hoped to get past it. He could already see that Stanley, who wore a particulate respirator mask, was eccentric, chose his words thoughtfully, carefully, and was not very revealing. What Alberto had imprinted, indelibly, front and center in his fine mind, was that Stanley was by far his most important client. To date, Stanley had sent Alberto a little more than $300,000,000 to invest over time in several projects. The origins of this money were untraceable. Alberto knew that Stanley was an early investor in Microsoft, and that he went on to earn a fortune as a venture capitalist, acquiring little known tech startups, and, as some mentioned in confidence, an early investment in X (formerly Twitter). He was successful enough that he had access to other large investors, some of whom could have contributed significant amounts of this money. Alberto didn't know. Stanley moved his money around the world, investing it conservatively in other countries, which was consistent with his eccentric, secretive personality.

Alberto did know that the money that came to the Cayman Island bank account arrived from very different places—Hong Kong, Luxembourg, Belize, Singapore—to name a few. It always ended up in the bank Alberto recommended to him in the Cayman Islands. He'd created a subsidiary account in the bank designed to service Stanley's investments exclusively. The size of each investment varied from $25,000,000 to $40,000,000, never more. The total of slightly more than $300,000,000 had arrived in ten separate deposits in the first year and a half. Each investment arrived as an untraceable shell corporation. Each deposit left the bank in a new shell corporation, so wherever it was eventually invested, the investor was untraceable. That was Stanley's first non-negotiable instruction to Alberto—he never, ever, wanted anyone to know who his investors were. On documents, the owner was always a different combination of several shell corporations. Five years ago, he'd instructed Alberto to invest his money in startup real estate developments. He'd decided to acquire them in and around Naples. Along the way, he'd approved two other developments — one in Fort Myers and another on Marcos Island. These developments which had been carefully built, and expanded over time, had prospered.

Once the developments were underway, Stanley received a quarterly statement which he always discussed with Alberto on the phone. He never got involved in the management of the developments, overseeing that was Alberto's job. Alberto had suggested several managers, and Stanley had approved one of his suggestions for each development. The manager oversaw existing houses, often sold some time ago, and new houses under development or as yet undeveloped. Alberto supervised each manager and regularly reported to Stanley. Alberto received a generous fee and 1 and 1/2 percent of the profits for his efforts. Twice a year, Stanley got a distribution into yet another shell corporation which was deposited in yet another account in Alberto's Cayman Island bank. As such, the investors, and the earnings from the investments, were untraceable.

"It's a pleasure to have a chance to talk in person," Alberto said.

"Yes," Stanley replied, quietly.

"I'm sorry we got off to an unexpectedly, unfortunate start. After your call, I contacted a senior man on the police force who will find the location of the people you need to reach."

"I hope so. As I told you on the phone, this incident has troubled me, deeply."

"I understand, and I intend to correct it. As I said, I barely know this man who took the photo. I have no idea how or why this happened."

Stanley looked up at Alberto. "Counselor, truthfully, that's not acceptable. I repeat — how is it possible that this could have ever, ever happened? How is it possible that a man you barely know would be in a position to take a photo of us without my permission?"

"There is no excuse. As I said, you have my sincere apologies. I will find this man, deal with him, and deal with the photo."

"You're too late for that. Here's what has already happened — my men saw him, followed him to the airport where he gave a flash drive to a journalist coming in on a plane... A well-known journalist - a man whose articles, I now know, have appeared in the *Miami Herald*, *The Times* in London, even the *New York Times*..."

"I'm sorry, sir, I am."

"Your apology is useless... My men dealt with your photographer, then found, interrogated, and, when he couldn't provide the photo, removed the journalist... the troubling problem is that they still haven't recovered the photo. Are you understanding how serious this is?"

"Yes, I think so."

"Has your man found anything yet."

"He has yet to report back."

Stanley stood, though he spoke quietly, anyone who knew him would see that he was patiently, forcefully, dictating his directives. "You need to do better... much better... Right away... Call him back, now. Tell him to get as much additional help as he needs. Money is not an object… Tell him he must find them today. Offer him whatever he needs. Write this down – **whatever he needs...**"

Alberto nodded, grimly, he got it. He picked up the phone. "Tom, I have to find that location today. Yes, right away… It's absolutely urgent… This is a more serious, a more important favor than I have ever asked you for… Get as much extra help as you need… Don't hesitate to use whatever resources you choose… I'll pay for the very best… There will be a handsome reward for you… Tom, lives are at stake… Post people to watch any place that even one of them might go to… Report back to me every hour."

Stanley nodded. "Well done… My purpose of meeting you, of this visit, was to further expand our work together. Unfortunately, the situation has changed for the worse… As such, I've been thinking about this very carefully and have come to a decision… Listen carefully… Unless and until you find them, and we recover all of the photos — that means any conceivable copies ever, past, present or possible to create in the future — unless and until that happens, I won't do any further business with you. If this isn't successfully resolved, I will hire someone to oversee, to supervise your work, to take charge of each and every detail. This kind of mistake should never, ever have happened. Period. And if it isn't corrected, timely, the consequences will be grave." Stanley stood up and turned to leave. "Am I perfectly clear?"

Alberto stood, distressed. "Yes, you're clear. I'll find them…"

"I'm sorry that we have to postpone our lunch and our conversation about the future, but under the circumstances, there's no alternative."

Alberto nodded. "Mr. White, I understand. Still, I want to reiterate that this is, for me, a very important professional relationship. While you're here, what else can I do to restore our heretofore excellent working relationship? Anything at all."

"There's nothing. Until you accomplish what I have demanded, there's nothing at all that you can do for me." Stanley left.

****

The Macher and Andre had joined the group in the living room. Andre got to NYC last night and arrived this morning with the Macher on his private jet. When they arrived, Cash, Callie, Alvaro, Sara, Miguel and Rafael had all contributed to filling them in on what they knew and all that had happened since Luis arrived. Now they were all listening as the Macher explained what he'd learned from his friend, the retired Venezuelan General, Mario Lopez.

"General Lopez was, at first, reluctant to even talk about this. He explained that it's still a sore subject, that truthfully, it's become a festering, infected open wound. It was a disaster when they lost three hundred and fifty million dollars, but it's inconceivable, an unprecedented catastrophe, that the military, with all of the resources, including the government, haven't recovered a dime - not one dime - after five years.

General Lopez knew General Gabriel Castillo, the suspected thief. He knew he had access to military funds, huge amounts of it, so yes, General Castillo could have stolen the money, but where had it gone? How was it moved? Who has it now? General Castillo had died soon after the money disappeared, which made recovery even more difficult.

Lopez, who was candid when he did agree to talk, explained that several years ago he left Venezuela choosing voluntary exile, living in Buenos Aires, Argentina, when he was no longer able to support the dictator who illegally claimed the presidency of Venezuela, despite global condemnation of a rigged election in 2019.

After he left Venezuela, someone anonymously floated the possibility that he, General Lopez, could possibly have been involved in the theft. General Lopez, who was appalled and enraged by that suggestion, reached out to his many colleagues and loyal friends to refute it, categorically. Since the explanation of his innocence was absolutely convincing, and since he was in fact, uninvolved, the speculation never went any further. However, since General Lopez had, in fact, worked with and had access to one of the foreign banks from which the military money disappeared, albeit legally, and since he had left the country it wasn't entirely forgotten. The Macher dismissed it as politically motivated garbage, and confirmed how respected he was—still—among high status Venezuelans, both in the military and elsewhere. He went further to reiterate how much he personally respected General Lopez for his political convictions, his refusal to recognize the current president as the legitimate president of Venezuela, which he, and many other foreign governments, including the United States, have expressed. He added how very much he liked him personally. That was more than enough for everyone in this conversation.

When the Macher was finished, Cash went back to the earlier question about the missing money, asking, "What if Gabriel had a friend, or a relative here who's putting the money into Florida real estate?"

"Do we have any evidence at all of that?" the Macher asked.

"No, none at all."

Alvaro offered, "It's just a guess based on Luis, Miguel's son, the journalist." He pointed at Miguel, sitting on a chair at the table. "Luis spent three months doing research and he kept notes that we still haven't read completely. He had some preliminary ideas based on his research, on the amount of Venezuelan money that's moved into Miami. He was interested in Alberto Leon as a starting point, based on his experience, albeit on a different scale, of moving money, because his name came up in another context, because he wasn't taking on new clients, and because Luis' father had access. And in the past twenty-four hours all of this has been fueled by how people are willing to kill to get that photo back."

Andre offered, "I talked with the Colonel I worked with. He's as clueless as Itzac's General. He also said that because of the tension between Venezuela and the US, the Venezuelan military can't do much to investigate anything here, certainly something as tentative, as unproven, as this."

"Will your General, Itzac, or your Colonel, Andre, help us?" Cash asked.

The Macher nodded. "General Lopez will look at the photo. If it's a friend or a relative of Gabriel Castillo, and he can recognize it, he'll jump right on it. The problem is that the masked man in the photo is pretty much unrecognizable…

That said, this missing money is still a huge deal for him, and it's important personally."

Andre added, "My Colonel made a point of reminding me that over the last five years, they've followed up lots of theories and many so-called clues that went nowhere, absolutely nowhere. No one is going to get excited unless we have more than a virtually unrecognizable photo."

The Macher nodded, "My friend, the General, went further. It's not enough to have a plausible theory. They have to be able to get the money back from the US, an unfriendly country. Even if you're right, it's virtually impossible to get legally invested money out of an expensive Florida real estate development just because the Venezuelan military is missing three hundred and fifty million dollars."

"So why are they killing people to get this photo?" Sara asked.

"To begin to answer that, it would help to know the man in the photo," the Macher replied.

"Yes, and we're working on that, as is Rafael. For now, Itzac, send the photo to the General today. Andre, send it to your Colonel. Rafael will get answers today or tomorrow. We may get lucky. Until then, I have another starting point." Cash went on, "There are two men in the photo, and one of them is identifiable. Let's see if we can learn more about Alberto Leon… I'd like it if you and Andre could spend time on that, right away. I'm also interested in learning more about the real estate developments. Miguel knows something about him and about the real estate, he'll help. In the meantime, Sara, Callie and I will go over Luis's notes. Alvaro, can you and Rafael go back to all of the break-in sites, and see if we missed anything?"

Rafael and Alvaro nodded, as did Andre and the Macher, agreeing to their assignments.

Cash thought of one further thing, "Miguel, can you call and ask someone in Alberto's office if he or she can give you the name of the man in the mask that Alberto was meeting? We need that now and should send it with the photo. Rafael, you should pass it on to the people who already have the photo."

Miguel nodded. "I know Alberto's secretary. I always bring her documents. She'll know. I'll call right away."

"One more thing. Rafael, stop off and talk with the police lieutenant who wanted to know where we are. Check him out."

"I intend to, I'll stop by the station on our way back. You know, I sent the photo to three able men who meet your requirements. I should begin hearing from them this afternoon."

"Good... It's eleven a.m., let's get the name, send the photo and regroup here at two p.m."

****

Cash, Callie, and Sara had been going over Luis's notes for almost an hour. Sara had found their first clue – apparently Luis had gotten independently to Alberto Leon. He'd researched the Venezuelan bank that the oil company used. He knew that the military had several accounts with the oil company. First, he went to a friend, a sophisticated Venezuelan banker with another bank. His friend talked with several colleagues in the oil company's bank. They didn't know anything about the whereabouts of the money in the accounts that had disappeared five years ago. All anyone, including the military and government investigators, knew was that about six or seven years ago, over about eighteen months, all of the money in the Venezuelan military accounts went into maximum high security accounts in Panama and Geneva, and from there, inexplicably, they were sent to multiple little known investment accounts in different locations. These monies deposited in these investment accounts were deposited by shell corporations. When investigators finally got to those accounts, they no longer existed, the money was gone, lost, impossible to trace. They'd all been interrogated many times by high level military investigators. They'd all told what they knew, which was little or nothing, and they had nothing to add.

One of them, however, mentioned that recently one of his clients wanted to move some money out of Venezuela. It was a small legal transaction and he'd gotten a name from a friend who had done this successfully for him eight or nine years ago. His friend had recommended a little-known lawyer in Miami, Florida, an international lawyer named Alberto Leon. For whatever reason, likely the request was too small, it never worked out for his client. Luis, however, was curious. He recognized the name, and he knew his father did some work for him. It wasn't much at all, but it was a place to start.

Luis, a smart reporter, started investigating just what Alberto Leon did. He contacted his dad, Miguel, to help. Miguel explained that Alberto had a relatively small practice, no criminal record, and that Alberto was only taking a few new clients because he was helping an important client who was investing in and managing several real estate developments. Nothing odd about that. It was not unheard of for a lawyer to help with a client's real estate investments. But then, two weeks later, Luis called him, using another name, asking if Alberto might handle a large transaction. His secretary said that he wasn't taking new clients. That was odd, Luis thought. Luis pressed on saying that he'd like to talk with him. His secretary said he was taking a trip and doubted if he'd want to talk, but she'd ask, and she took Luis' number. That night, when his father called with more research information, Luis just asked where Alberto was going. His father knew that he was going to the Cayman Islands. Apparently, he went there once or twice a year to meet with a bank that he did a lot of business with. Luis nodded, interested that Alberto wasn't taking on new business and interested in his regular visits to the Cayman Islands.

Later, Callie noticed that Luis had gotten hold of a military investigation report of the disappearance. All that they knew was that the Venezuelan oil company's military account had multiple accounts in Switzerland and Panama, two maximum high secrecy places. General

Gabriel Castillo was authorized to move money in and out of those accounts. Over about eighteen months, he transferred ten separate items of $25,000,000–$40,000,000 each into five of the regular company accounts. They were characterized as acquisitions for normal military requirements. Nothing about them was unusual. In total it was over $300,000,000. Those pieces never arrived at their assigned sellers. In short, they disappeared. The Swiss and Panama banks refused to disclose the destinations. Under extreme legal pressure from the Venezuelan military and government, they simply ended the conversation, saying they'd been instructed to send all of the money in separate large pieces to multiple investment accounts in different locations. When investigators finally got to those accounts they no longer existed, the money was gone, lost, impossible to trace. The investment company couldn't be found.

The investigator had one admittedly, far-fetched theory. He suggested that General Gabriel Castillo could have used a Hawalader to transfer the money further. Callie learned that Hawala, which means trust, was an underground banking system whereby money can be made available internationally without actually moving it or leaving a record of the transactions. One Hawalader could send a message to another who would cover the money and repay it from outstanding transactions. The brokers are neither licensed nor supervised. Hawaladers were known to move hundreds of millions of dollars. The investigators suggested that General Gabriel must have spent a long time finding a capable, trustworthy Hawalader and once he put the money in his hands, there was no possible way of tracing it. He postulated that the bogus investment accounts were skillfully created by shell corporations in the Hawalader's network, who quickly began moving it expertly, untraceably, without any record of the transactions. At the end of their report, the investigators said, "To put it clearly, Hawal provides total anonymity in its transactions, as official records aren't kept and the source of money can't be tracked. There is no longer any possible way to find the missing $350,000,000. No way whatsoever." It was, Callie thought, the perfect crime.

****

The Macher and Andre were frustrated. As much as they could tell from Miguel, the real estate developments were flawless, squeaky clean. Alberto Leon insisted that every rule was obeyed, every detail was observed. Every "I" was dotted, every "T" was crossed. Okay, they'd also learned that the contact in the investments was Stanley White, the masked man in the photo. He, apparently, wanted it done exactly that way. Furthermore, there was a lot more work to be done. Though they were all selling well, only about half of the houses were built, and that meant a lot more money was going in than coming out. The Macher did the math—it cost about $600,000 to build an average unit that sold for $800,000. That means the maximum profit, without other costs is $200,000. Including other costs, like buying the land, administrating and maintaining the development, sales costs, security, office staff, permits, taxes, etc. He guessed the total profit at about $100,000 per unit. So, if they'd built and sold seventy units that means they'd made $7,000,000. They're still pouring in $30,000,000 in future building, that is to say fifty more units, and that was just the one development. If his math was right, they were $23,000,000 in the red on just one development. He multiplied that by three and considered that one development would have 300 units or 180 more than the others. The Macher calculated that after investing in at least the first $200,000,000, they were more than $150,000,000 behind. He stood, then concluded, "If they had almost three hundred and fifty million to invest, they likely had plans to build even more developments, perhaps they'd already invested in more land, more developments. This is an estimate, but I'd guess their three hundred and fifty million will be under water for fifteen or twenty years."

Andre asked, "Why steal three hundred and fifty million dollars and piss it away for twenty years. Whoever is behind this will be dead before they make any real money."

The Macher nodded. "Think about that carefully. It's precisely what I would do." The Macher smiled. "First, you make the money disappear—which they obviously did extremely well. But then you don't want anyone to find it. What's better than hiding it in real estate developments for twenty years? You don't need any more large sums of money during those years, and you can always regularly take enough amounts of money that you might need out of existing developments. Who would ever suspect that these cash poor, long-term developments are being funded with stolen money?"

"Some crackpot like you would suspect it."

"That's why you like me."

"Who said I like you?"

"Well, you are listening to me."

"Yes, and truthfully, I take your point. Still, we have absolutely no proof."

Miguel just stared at these two guys.

Andre repeated, "There's not even a shred of evidence—"

Miguel interrupted, angry, "They killed my son. What more do you need?"

The Macher replied, "We're sorry. We didn't mean to be insensitive, but if we're going back to a Venezuelan General, even a retired General, and asking him for help, I need to give him some realistic chance of recovering their money."

Miguel nodded. "I have an idea."

****

After checking out his nightclub and his house, and finding nothing new, Alvaro went with Rafael to the police station. Rafael suggested that Alvaro wait in the car outside, which he did. Inside, Rafael found the Lieutenant, Tom Franklin, who had been trying to reach them.

Tom Franklin had been polite, but he was not happy when Rafael said that the others had moved to another location, and he didn't know where they were. He explained that he hadn't wanted to know where. Lieutenant Franklin had pulled rank. He ordered Rafael, angrily, to find out, right away. He insisted that time was of the essence. Rafael lied, and said he'd do what he could.

When he came out Alvaro was gone.

Rafael drove around the parking lot, went back inside to check the bathrooms, even asked a couple of other policemen if they'd seen a man walking in the parking lot. Nothing. Sensing the worst, he called Cash.

"I'm at the police station. I left Alvaro in the car, when I came out, he was gone. Did he call you? Is that like him to take off?"

"No, they got him. Come back here, right away. You left him in the car alone? I expected better from you."

"I thought he'd be safe in the police station parking lot. But I've got no excuse. I screwed up, period."

"Yes, you did. Damnit!" Cash hung up.

****

Back at the house, Cash had told everyone, except Sara, who was sleeping, that Alvaro was missing. It felt like déjà vu, and Cash was furious with himself and very worried about how Sara would take it when she woke up. Before he could rant or even start to make a plan, the phone rang. He was expecting it, and he picked it right up.

"Who is this?" the unknown voice, one of Stanley's men, asked.

"My name is Cash. The man you have, Alvaro, is my son-in-law."

"He will die if you don't give us the photo and convince us, without a shadow of a doubt, that there are no copies left, or any other copies outstanding, anywhere."

"If we do that, will you simultaneously return him safely?"

"If and only if you've met our requirements. They must be met perfectly. We will need absolute certainty that the photo, or any copy of the photo past or present no longer exists. If any copies have been given to others, you'll have to retrieve them and destroy them. This may be difficult, but it's non-negotiable. We will also require proof positive that future copies can never be created."

The Macher and Andre nodded, emphatically. Cash didn't hesitate. "I will agree to that, and I will convince you that your demands have been met. I have one further condition."

The Macher nodded, again, signaling Cash that he would handle this, then responded, "This is Itzac. I am Cash's partner in this matter. I speak for all of us. If Alvaro isn't returned safely. If he's harmed at all, in any way, we will hunt you down and kill you… Every last one of you… That's a promise."

"Ah… You sound like an old man… You'd be wise not to make threats you can't accomplish… you'd be better off spending your time making sure that you meet all of our demands perfectly. If not, you'll never see your friend Alvaro again."

The Macher sighed. "Yes, I am an old man. However, I am an old man that has always kept his promises… Always, without fail… Alvaro lives or you and your associates die horrific deaths… We'll give you the photo, and the proof that you need at 9:00 a.m. tomorrow morning provided that you give us Alvaro–alive and well. Are we in agreement?"

"Yes, we will make this exchange at his nightclub. nine a.m. No surprises. It will be on you to convince me that there is no possible way that anyone else will ever see this photo. If I'm convinced, and only if, we will return Alvaro. And old man, if you ever threaten me again, you will taste my wrath." He hung up.

"How are you going to convince them?" Callie asked.

Cash made a face. "We can destroy the original flash drive photo, erase my computer, destroy the copies on Itzac and Andre's phones, have Rafael recall the three he sent out, and I can truthfully say that there's no possible way to recreate that photo. They still won't believe that the photo no longer exists."

The Macher nodded. "That's because if they had it, they'd keep a copy."

"Right. They'll keep Alvaro," Andre said.

"Not necessarily," Cash said. "Not if we've got something else to trade."

"Such as?"

"Miguel, can you find their location?"

"When I called Alberto's secretary, Janine, to find his name, I asked after, if she knew where Stanley White stays when he's in Miami. Apparently, he lives on a large yacht and moves around often. She guessed that today he'd be on an island nearby."

"That could be anywhere. Can you find out precisely where?"

"I can try. I have to go there, bring Janine some signed documents. I'll see what I can find out."

The Macher spoke up. "Get one of Stanley's people on the boat's cell phone number, any way that you can. Distract Janine and look in her phone list, her Rolodex, whatever. She surely has a listing for Stanley's assistant. That's all I need to pinpoint the location."

"I'm sure they have it – his name is Erik - so I'll find it. One way or another."

"Okay. Let's assume you can." Cash paused, looked around at each of them, serious, preoccupied now. He turned to Andre. "Hear me out—this is hardball. Andre, you'll get this right away. Once we have found that boat, tonight, I want you to plant at least four explosives - I don't need to detail that for you. I'll want you to be able to detonate them, one at a time, at my signal during the 9:00 a.m. meeting. I have to be able to trigger an explosion from Alvaro's nightclub."

Andre nodded. "We find the boat; I can do that."

"The first blast shouldn't sink it or kill anyone. It's a warning. After that, each one should be systematic, unmitigated destruction at different specified locations."

The Macher stood. "Miguel, go find the phone number. Right away."

At the door Miguel turned. "I'll keep you posted. I don't want any more of us to die."

Callie called out, "Godspeed." She turned to Cash. "We need to tell Sara. Do you want me to go with you?"

"Yes, thank you. This is going to be a nightmare."

****

Sara was sleeping in a downstairs bedroom. Her son was asleep beside her on the bed. Cash and Callie crept in, softly. They took one look and went back outside. They went together down the hall and into another bedroom, then closed the door behind them. Callie was crying. Cash took her in his arms, then he was tearing up, too. After a minute he stepped back, used his handkerchief to wash away her tears, then his own.

"I don't think we should tell her," Cash whispered. "I'm not sure she'll be able to handle it."

"I had the same reaction," Callie nodded. "What can we do?"

"I don't know."

"If we don't tell her, we damn well better bring her husband home tomorrow morning, safely."

"That's what I intend to do."

"She'll still be really, really angry."

"Yes, I know, but it will be better for her than worrying every minute he's gone that he's going to die."

"What if I take her and the baby away somewhere tonight?"

"That's a good idea. I'll find a safe place."

"Can you invent some story that Alvaro is going to be with you doing something tonight?"

"I will. I'll think of something. The Macher will help. He's good at that."

"You mean lying."

"No, I mean making other people feel good, even if it's not exactly true."

"Right, of course... Are we weak, even cowardly? You know that if anything happens to Alvaro; she'll never forgive us."

"No, I'll live by our decision... Hell, there's no good choice... I think sparing Sara until we have him back is the best we can do."

Callie took him in her arms again, kissed him tenderly. After a moment, she stepped back. "I'm worried about this... But I love you, Cash Logan."

****

Miguel called from outside Alberto's office. "I have Erik, Stanley assistant's cell phone number," he said, when Cash answered.

Cash gave the phone to the Macher, who wrote it down, then said, "Thanks. That's all I need. Take the night off. I'll call you tomorrow, after we get Alvaro back."

"Godspeed. I'll be thinking about you."

"Thank you."

The Macher put the cell phone number in his tracker and located the large yacht in the Marcos Island Yacht Club. The marina where the yacht was tied up was just to the right over the S.S. Jolley Bridge as you drive onto the island. Cash and the Macher identified the yacht on Google Maps, then passed it on to Andre. Andre agreed to get the equipment he needed, then take the drive to the island and locate the boat. He had his scuba gear and after sunset, he'd swim under the boat and place the explosives.

After Andre left, Cash and Callie explained to the Macher that they'd decided not to tell Sara that her husband had been kidnapped.

"That's thoughtful," he offered right away. "I hope it works out... She's got enough to worry about without fearing for her husband's life. What are you going to tell her?"

"That's what we wanted to talk with you about," Callie replied. "I thought I'd take her and the baby someplace safe, but Cash suggested that you'd be helpful coming up with a story about what Alvaro was doing."

"You mean I've become the expert liar?"

"Something like that."

"Well, I'll take that as a compliment... Okay, tell her that since the police lieutenant called, we don't think this is a safe place to be. That's why you're taking her and the baby away tonight. Then you can explain that Cash, Alvaro and I are meeting with Miguel—he has an idea of how we can interest my friend, the Venezuelan General. Later, we'll meet with a man the General's already sent to hear our plan. We'll need Alvaro's

Spanish for that meeting. If you need more, tell her that if we have time, the three of us are also checking out several boats I've located that we can rent. With any luck at all we can move tonight… Is that enough?"

"Is any of that true?"

Cash replied, "Sweetheart, it's all partly true, or close enough, that's what makes him so good at this."

****

Callie and Cash went back into Sara's room where they woke her up. When they finished carefully telling her the entire plan, she looked first at Callie, then at her dad, and then spread out both arms, hands up, facing them, pushing them away, as she burst into tears.

Through her tears she cried out, "What happened? You guys are lousy fucking liars! Is Alvaro in danger?"

Callie looked at Cash, then she started to cry, too.

Cash said, "Yes, we didn't want to frighten you, but Alvaro has been kidnapped."

Sara screamed.

The baby was up now. Callie took him, held him, rocked him gently.

Cash went on. "We have a plan to get him back tomorrow morning. I think it will work. They want to trade him for the photo. We mistakenly thought we could spare you from this."

"God fucking damnit!... Damnit! Damnit! Damnit!"

Callie took Y.C., unsettled, on her lap, then turned, still crying, to Sara, "…we're so sorry… It seemed like the humane choice."

"Don't ever, ever do anything like that again. Never, ever! I can manage terrifying worry. I can deal with knowing something terrible has happened. What I can't tolerate, ever… is my family, my closest friends, lying to me about it…" She yelled, "Am I clear? Am I fucking well clear?" She took a slow breath, then reached out to take her unhappy child.

Cash touched Sara's arm gently, watching her calm her son. "Yes… Yes, sweetheart, you're clear…"

"I meant what I said. When I made you give up your work and we agreed to a plan to try to keep this from happening, it never, ever included lying to me. How could you do that?"

"It was bad judgement … We made a mistake… Let's come back to why and what we were thinking later. Let's focus on what we're planning to do to get him back. We intend to do that… Please focus on that."

"Dad, don't break my heart and then tell me what to focus on."

"Okay… I'm sorry… I'm not sure how to fix this… I'm not used to making this kind of mistake." He took his daughter in his arms, softly saying. "I never, ever want to hurt you… I'm sure I speak for Callie as well. Will you please forgive us… I do have a plan to get Alvaro back. I would, at least, like to tell you about it."

"I'm beside myself with worry. Inside, I'm burning up… This plan better be goddamn good…" Sara had sat Y.C. on a blanket on the floor. He seemed happy, as she gave him his truck on the blanket. Sara turned back to her dad and Callie. Her face was weary, despondent. "It has to work—has to—or my life is over…"

****

Andre saw the luxurious Sunseeker 116 Yacht, the Island Voyager, tied up at the furthest dock at the northeast end of the Marcos Island Yacht Club. Going over the Jolley Bridge, the Yacht Club is just to your right. Under the bridge to the left, there was a fishing area with unpaved parking. The location was perfect for his purpose. He chose a secluded parking spot, then walked to a protected space from which he could see the yacht. With his powerful binoculars, he took a careful look at the Sunseeker 116 Yacht. It was, he thought, spacious and luxurious, with multiple guest cabins, suitable for extended cruising in international waters. He focused his high-powered binoculars on the aft deck. He recognized Stanley White from the photo. He still wore a mask. There were several other men with him that Andre didn't know. Pleased to confirm the right boat, he walked slowly toward the Yacht Club. He identified several spots where he could enter the water at night, unseen, then swim below the boat. When he was satisfied, he went back to his car. Andre slowly drove off toward town, where he found a simple Italian restaurant with homemade pizza, where he could wait comfortably.

****

On the boat, Stanley White had gathered his crew to eat dinner together on the aft deck to go over, then finalize their plan. There were now six of them sitting around the table, including Stanley. There were two highly trained killers, Ruben and Carlos - who'd found and killed Luis and his helper, Garcia, then attacked Sara and searched Alvaro's nightclub and later their house. Ruben and Carlos were first trained, then served—before Stanley recruited them—in high positions in the Venezuelan General Directorate of Military Counterintelligence (Direccion General de Contrainteligencia Militar, or DGCIM). DGCIM is part of the armed forces but serves at the pleasure of the president and is responsible for (among other things) neutralizing threats to the current power structure, including dissent within military ranks. In 2019, the US Treasury sanctioned the DGCIM for its violence, including the assassination of a captain in the Venezuelan Navy. Years ago, when he'd spent time in Venezuela, Stanley had been a friend and a financial advisor to well-known politicians and several military officers. That's how he'd had access to recruit high level DGCIM trained men.

The others at the table were Tim, his own trusted, long-term business and financial expert; Erik, who had become Stanley's administrative assistant. Erik had been mostly running odd jobs and personal errands for many years; and finally, Johan, the captain of the yacht's cook. Stanley waited until Johan described their dinner, a favorite, a Mediterranean lamb and lentil stew, then everyone served themselves. After listening to enthusiastic praise for the dinner, Stanley began. "Are we ready to finalize our plan tomorrow morning?" He asked.

"Yes," Ruben replied. "We'll hear them out, take the photos they offer, get whatever proof they can put forward, then keep the hostage."

“Is it possible that they will return all of the photos, eliminate every possibility of the photos ever being duplicated?” Tim asked.

“We’ve considered that. Suppose they did? How could we be sure?” Erik asked.

Ruben nodded. “I think our plan is the ***only*** way. If we keep the hostage, it will make it their responsibility to convince us.”

Stanley looked around the table, seeing agreement, then concluded, “As we’ve said, let’s tell them that we intend to keep the hostage until they’ve met our demands persuasively. Time is our ally. Soon after we say that, I’m certain that they’ll find a way to satisfy us to get their friend, husband and the child’s father back. Once we have that, we can safely move on. Sometime later, and discretely, we’ll kill them all.”

****

Andre enjoyed his pizza, then called Cash. “I’ve found it, picked a good spot to enter the water, and I’ll set the explosives after dark.”

“Good. Please walk me through your plan.”

“I’m thinking I’ll go back tonight and park among the fisherman just under the bridge. The fishermen will be finished by dark. I’ll carry my equipment in a duffel to a remote spot I’ve chosen where I can get ready then quietly slip into the water. After I set the explosives, I’ll go back to a motel I found in town. In the morning, I’ll go back to my parking area. There’s a spot where I can watch and wait for your call. I’ll wait until you give me a signal, then I’ll detonate the bomb on the nose of the boat. I want to see the explosive go off. I can detonate that explosion easily and unnoticed from my spot under the bridge. I can detonate a second explosion from the same spot if you decide that’s necessary.”

After eating dessert, cherry pie, Andre drove his car back to the parking area. After dark, just past 9:30 p.m., it was empty. He carried the duffel with his scuba gear and another carefully packed, waterproof container with his other equipment. At his chosen isolated spot, he put on his scuba gear. Next, he took his packed waterproof bag with the explosive and the other equipment he needed, attached them at his waist, entered the water and swam under water toward the boat. He'd learned long ago to swim effectively with one prosthetic leg. A little after an hour later, he'd set four plastic explosives—one smaller, near the nose and just above the water, designed to cause cosmetic damage, and three larger bombs, under the vessel, positioned to cause serious structural damage. He swam back to his spot, took off and packed up his scuba gear, then he walked to the car, put his scuba gear and his other remaining equipment in the trunk, then drove to the local motel he'd found in town not far from the restaurant.

CHAPTER THREE

Cash was in Alvaro's nightclub, sitting at a table near the door with the Macher, Sara, who had her baby playing on a blanket at her feet, and Callie. The policeman, Rafael, had wanted to be there but Cash said no, for obvious reasons. Rafael didn't need to know what they intended to do. Rafael did, however, report that none of his people recognized the man in the photo. Cash had told him to retrieve the photos and sit tight until they could talk tomorrow.

At precisely 9:00 a.m., Cash's phone rang. "You know why we're calling," the voice said. It was Erik, Stanley's righthand man.

"We have the flash drive of the photo, the computer I downloaded it on, all three of the cell phones that had it. We have retrieved three copies that we sent out. There are no other copies of the photo. None."

"How can we be certain of that?"

"We kept no other copies. I can guarantee you that," Cash insisted.

"Put them outside, in front of the door, then close the door again and we'll examine them."

"Before we turn these over, we need to see Alvaro."

"We'll bring him outside in front. You can see him from a distance, but we won't release him before we examine the photos and we're convinced."

With a gesture, Sara gave her son to Callie, then Cash and Sara, still injured, moving uneasily, came running out the front door. A car was parked there, in front. Ruben opened the back door. Sara recognized Ruben, though she didn't know his name. Ruben lifted Alvaro out to lean against the car. Alvaro was handcuffed and gagged, but apparently unharmed.

Sara started to cry. Cash held her back. Cash put the photo, the computer, and all three phones on the front entryway, then he led Sara back inside.

Inside, Cash called Andre on another phone. "Get ready for the first explosion on my signal."

"I'm in position, waiting for your instruction."

"Okay, I'm leaving this phone open. I'm guessing it won't be long. My signal is 'PLASTIC.'" Cash left the phone on, set it on the table.

Everyone else was waiting, anxiously, around the table. Several minutes later, Cash's other phone rang.

"We have examined the material. We are not convinced that you haven't made and kept other copies."

"How can we convince you of that?"

"That's your problem." The Macher had opened the door, and they could see the car leaving. "We're keeping your friend until you can solve that problem and convince us, without any possible doubt."

"Please stay on the phone," Cash instructed.

Cash spoke into the other phone, "PLASTIC."

The nose of the yacht exploded. Cash imagined hearing it from where they were, then speaking into the other phone, "Call your boss. The front of his yacht just exploded. Unless you return our friend, Alvaro, unharmed, RIGHT NOW, there will be a series of explosions each one destroying your boat further, until it no longer exists." He could hear Erik, talking on the other phone. Cash interrupted, "the next explosion will do structural damage and begin sinking your yacht. Give us Alvaro NOW!"

Ruben took over. "You sons of bitches are bluffing. We'll kill him before we release him now."

Cash spoke into the second phone again, "PLASTIC," he said again.

The next explosion was louder still. Andre watched a piece of the boat fly into the air as water came in and a fire spread onto the yacht.

****

Stanley was screaming into the phone, "Damnit, I live on this boat… Ruben, give them back the hostage!"

Johan arrived. He had a fire extinguisher that he aimed at the flames. It didn't extinguish the fire. Stanley grabbed another extinguisher, expertly causing the flames to subside, then he yelled at Johan, "Get this fire out, right away, then get Tim, go downstairs, stop the leaking water. Don't make me say it again."

Johan emptied his extinguisher, then when the fire had been slowed, he finished Stanley's extinguisher. He yelled into his phone to Tim, who was downstairs. "How bad is it? I'll be right there."

Cash jumped in, saying, matter of fact, "Stanley, if you return Alvaro RIGHT NOW, you can still save your yacht. The next explosion will be far worse… You have less than thirty seconds."

Stanley spoke to Cash, "He's on his way…" then yelling, "Ruben, I SAID NOW!"

Cash took a good look at Ruben as he opened the door after the car stopped in front. Alvaro was roughly thrown out the door, still handcuffed, then Ruben was back inside, and the car was gone.

Cash and Sara, moving uneasily, hurried out to help Alvaro. Once he was up, they helped him to the house, laying him on the couch. Callie was playing with Y.C. on the floor. The Macher sat beside Alvaro, using a tool to unlock his handcuffs. Sara carefully brought him some water, then gingerly put her arm around him.

She whispered, "I was so scared…Sweetheart, I can't live without you."

Alvaro kissed her, tenderly.

Cash interrupted. "We have to move quickly. They'll come after us. They'll want payback, right away. They have to know that we're inching closer, so I'd bet that they're past simply worrying about the photo. The'll kill us all if they can."

"Yes," the Macher agreed.

"Here's what I think we should do," Cash looked at everyone. "Today, right now, Sara, Alvaro, Y.C., and Callie should get on the

Macher's plane and go to Cuba and hide. I'll call Nestor and get him to meet you at the airport, get you in. He'll set you up in a safe place."

Callie turned. "I'll stay if I can help."

"Thank you, but this is a war, and Andre and the Macher are the experts at that. I know I can count on you if I need you, and if so, I'll let you know..." He turned to Callie, a long loving glance. "Babe, if we learned anything from our year at sea, it was to minimize our risk to loved ones until we have no choice. If and when we need to take that risk, we will. Until then, I want you to be safe."

"Okay, thank you, I get that. What about you?"

"The Macher is already finding a new safe house for us. He and Andre will look after me, they're good at that."

Both Sara and Callie looked at the Macher. Sara finally spoke. "Itzac, you were part of many of our conversations at sea. Do we need to go to war, yet again? Can we all just walk away from them?"

The Macher looked at Sara thoughtfully. "It won't work. We worried them, they rightly think we're a threat, and now, they intend to kill all of us. They're experienced professionals. Unless we stop them, they will eventually succeed. I've already contacted a former Venezuelan General, a friend, who's going to help us. I understand your concern, but we have to deal with this, we know how to do that, and we'll be careful."

Sara went on, unsatisfied, "This is not our fault. Alvaro's cousin, Luis, started it, unintentionally... and now, once again, I'm really worried about my dad. Why does that keep happening? How is that possible?"

Callie answered, "It's not what anyone wanted, but he's doing the right thing, the thing he has to do. He's taking this risk because he loves you, your son, and Alvaro so very much. And because of who he is. He and his friends can protect you. Now is a time to feel good, even proud, about that."

"You're right, and I do..." Sara started to cry. "But Goddammit, I hate this... I really hate it..."

"That's good," Callie said. "We all do. But for us, for now, it's part of living. Maybe it's bad luck, or fate, or something else we can't control. People who engage life with intensity, with passion, be it in their friendships, choosing lovers, raising children or simply taking on difficult work, they all take risks. Most of the time they're measured, carefully chosen and controllable – that's what we worked on at sea for a year. And, as we know, that can work most of the time. But imagine a sailboat, caught in an unexpected, life-threatening storm, or an experienced hiker, being stalked by a ferocious grizzly bear. What if your son was exposed to a lethal virus at an airport? Bad things happen to good people who didn't bring them on themselves. When that happens, you simply do your best. In your case, your best happens to be very damn good."

Sara took a slow breath, then looked at Callie. "Okay. I get it... Here's where you say to me—'Just fucking man up.'"

Callie smiled, put her arm around Sara. "If I was able to be as straightforward, as candid, as articulate as you, that's what I'd say."

****

Stanley and three of his people, Ruben and Carlos, the DCGIM special forces, and Erik, his trusted righthand, were at a coffee shop not far from the Yacht Club. Johan and Tim were still on the boat. They'd managed to temporarily contain the leak and now they had three experts preparing to tow the yacht into a boat repair service on the island. Stanley was prepared to go to the airport, and he was giving final instructions to his people.

"Carlos, as soon as we're finished here, I want you to drive Erik and me to the airport. I'm on an afternoon flight to San Francisco. I'll be at the vineyard tonight. I'll expect you to follow with Tim tomorrow. Johan will be responsible for the boat. Once we know the damage, and the timing to repair it, we'll decide on next steps. Ruben, I want you to stay here, and I'll expect you to inflict a measure of our vengeance as soon as possible. We'll come back to that. For now, suffice it to say that they are closer than anyone has gotten, and we'll have to go into hiding until this has blown over. It's also obvious that they're smart. They will also go into hiding and be difficult to find, harder still to kill. Nevertheless, we'll want to kill them in due course. They've come too far, and the photo is no longer our only problem. In the meantime, let them stew. They will have no way to find us, and while they're confused, Ruben, I want you to strike unexpectedly, viciously. Shock them. First, destroy their nightclub, total destruction, a raging fire and devastating explosions, then kill their accessible associates, both Miguel, the journalist Luis' father, and Rafael, the policeman who helped them. Those men should be findable, and the others, in hiding, will get the message. In the meantime, I'll work on a plan to flush out the hiding principals."

"How much do you think they know?"

"Though I don't know how, and they have no evidence, I'm concerned that they're curious about the real estate developments."

"How is that possible?"

"That's the worst case, and I have to assume it, but it's not certain. Luis had some unspecified reason to be interested in Alberto, and although Alberto doesn't know anything about what we're actually doing, he's a step closer to the real estate."

"Do you want me to eliminate Alberto?" Ruben asked.

"No. We still need him, and if necessary, I can use him to mislead them. If we kill him, that will bring Cash and his team down even harder on the real estate. They'll be able to bring in all kinds of police, FBI, money laundering experts, government agencies, and so on into this. For now, we'll disappear without a trace. Ruben, you can remind them, unforgettably, that even if they can't find us, even if they have no idea where we are, they're still in mortal danger."

****

Cash put Callie, Sara, Alvaro and Y.C. on the Macher's plane. It was noon. Although he was glad the Macher was taking them to Cuba, getting them in and setting them up safely with Nestor, he was also relieved that the Macher had hired a capable, younger pilot. Itzac was a fine pilot, but he was too old to be taking this precious cargo. Cash made sure everyone was comfortably seated and had what they needed for what could be a long stay. No one knew how long. Before getting off the plane, Cash went around hugging and kissing everyone goodbye, again, very aware that these were his favorite people in the world, and he didn't know when he'd see them again. He watched the plane take off, turn toward Cuba, then he called Andre. He confirmed that Andre would follow Stanley. Later, they would meet back at the new safe house that the Macher had somehow arranged in South Beach, above a small restaurant in an old art deco building.

Andre had followed Stanley and his group as they left Marcos Island. He saw Stanley and Erik, his righthand man, get dropped off at a fancy hotel near the airport. Though he waited almost two hours, they didn't come out. In fact, by the time Andre left for the safe house, Stanley and Erik were on their way to San Francisco.

In their hotel room, Stanley had changed his well-dressed clothes to casual slacks and a well-designed men's post-shoulder surgery shirt, changed his mask to a large bandage covering half of his face, and then he was wheeled out of the hotel in a wheelchair by Erik, dressed as a physician's assistant wearing a mask. Andre was there when they went out of the door to get a new driver in a car that was set up to take a wheelchair, but all he saw was an injured old man being carried in a wheelchair by a physician's assistant. He didn't recognize these people at all.

The safe house that the Macher had found was in a lively, art deco building—bright colors and pastels, lots of pink, aqua blue, and bright yellow. It was a relatively small, four-story building, with a simple, colorful Cuban restaurant on the first floor spreading out onto the sidewalk. There were two apartments on each floor, accessible from the side of the building. The Macher had managed to get both apartments on the third floor. These two apartments had been connected into one large spacious unit. Cash had no idea how he was able to do that, but he'd long since given up on guessing the Macher's connections and his ability to get things done quickly and discretely. All that Cash knew was that he'd rented the third-floor unit as Mr. Smithfield and had given

Cash two keys. Inside, Cash could see that the unit was comfortable, and that some basic groceries had been delivered and put away.

First thing, Cash sat on the counter and called Miguel. He'd called him earlier to tell him Alvaro was home, safe, but he didn't have time to go further. He'd promised he'd call later. Miguel had said he'd be back this afternoon, and they'd set their call for 3:00 p.m. Since putting his loved ones on a plane to Cuba, Cash had been worrying about him, thinking that he was a potential, accessible payback target.

When Miguel answered, Cash jumped right in, "Miguel, I should have taken more time earlier, but I had to hide my family. They're out of the country now, safe. Andre, the Macher and I are hiding out in a new safe house. I'll fill you in later. When we rescued Alvaro, we had to set off two explosions on Stanley's yacht, one did serious damage. We didn't sink it, but it's pretty beat up. I think Stanley is going to strike back at us soon, and I'm worried about your safety."

"I'm okay."

"Please bear with me. If these people want to hurt us, and you're the only one they can find easily, you're going to die. I want you to leave Florida, right away. Please, there's already been one tragic death in your family. I don't want another one. This whole deal is going very fast. Do you have family outside of Florida?"

"Yes, I have two nephews and their families in Dallas."

"Perfect. Go there right now. Get on a plane today. I don't want to take any chances. Will you promise me that?"

"Yes, I'll leave right away…"

"Keep me posted."

"Okay… You blew up the yacht? Blew up Stanley's yacht? Jesus, Cash. That's excellent...That's outstanding...Talk soon."

"You're a good man, Miguel. I'll be in touch." Cash turned off his phone.

Cash helped himself to a beer he'd found in the refrigerator. Next, he sat at the counter to drink and wait to hear from the Macher.

It was almost 2:30 p.m. He went over the day and felt pretty good about where they'd ended up.

Maybe an hour later, his phone rang. It was the Macher.

"All's well," he began. "Nestor did his usual great job organizing everything. I saw him at the airport. He said he found a comfortable old house, plenty of room for everyone, including a guest room for you. Sara and Alvaro are very happy to be back. At the airport, after Nestor produced some kind of document, he whisked everyone through customs, no questions asked. I said goodbye to everyone there, but not before Callie announced that she was making dinner for all of them, including Nestor's family. I left before she had the opportunity to convince me to stay. Callie's Cuban paella, believe me, I was tempted. I'm on my way to the plane now, then enroute to Miami."

"I'm at the South Beach apartment. You've done a pretty fair job yourself. Whose apartment is it?"

"You don't want to know…"

"Itzac…"

"Okay, I'll tell you, because I know that you won't be satisfied, that you'll be a total insufferable pest until I do."

"Smart," Cash said, "An older man's insight, even wisdom."

"You know what it is, a nudnik? An annoying person…" The Macher chuckled. "OK. His name is Jimmy Finley, people call him "Dodger," don't ask me why. He's an accomplished gemstone trader. He works in the most sophisticated international marketplaces such as India, Thailand, Brazil, even Zambia. I sold him some diamonds years ago. He was honest with me, and we liked each other. He bought the apartment, fixed it up for his mistress. Almost a year ago, he was sentenced to do two years in prison, convicted on some kind of tax evasion charge. While he was inside, the Dodger's girlfriend found another boyfriend. Jimmy found out and kicked her out, but he kept the apartment. In prison, he needed some help moving some money around. He was good to use diamonds, so I helped him do that. He owes me, and he's happy for us to use the apartment."

"You're telling me more than I want to know. I thought maybe you rented it."

"Are you kidding?... And are you ever satisfied, boychik?" The Macher snorted, an old man's grumpy sound. "On another subject, the retired Venezuelan General, Mario Lopez, arrives tomorrow. I think we should meet with him right away."

"Yes, good, first thing. Who else do we want at this meeting? Andre?"

"He's, of course, welcome, but I don't think we need him… I've been thinking about this. I think it would be most helpful to have Detective Rafael with us. If General Lopez agrees to help us, he'll have to deal with the tense relationship between Venezuela and the US It will only help to have an accomplished US police officer on our team."

"I'll call him now…What time tomorrow?"

"Ten a.m.… I'll set it up. Talk soon." Itzac hung up.

The phone rang again, Cash picked up. "Cash here."

"Cash, it's Detective Rafael. I have bad news. Alvaro's nightclub, the Midnight Mirage, it's been destroyed. It was set on fire and blown to pieces with powerful explosives. It's still burning, but there's nothing left. This was an unmistakable message."

"Damnit. I can be there in ten minutes."

"No. There's nothing you can do."

"Then, I'll send my man, Andre, right away. I'll need photos. Please wait for him. Answer his questions, he's smart. I need to reach Alvaro and Sara. I'll call you back. Oh, one more thing, right away, please put at least two police cars around their house. I'd bet that the nightclub is just act one."

Cash called Andre. "They destroyed the Midnight Mirage. They blew it up and burned it down."

"Bastards, they're fast."

"Yes. Experienced professionals and fast. Please go there now, Rafael is waiting for you. He'll tell you what he knows. When you've checked it out, call me. I've got to tell Alvaro and Sara."

"What about their house?"

"I told Rafael to put two cop cars on it. You should still check it out later, make sure it's safe."

****

Stanley White, a.k.a. Brendan Dubois, sat comfortably in his wheelchair, resting on the patio overlooking his 1,100-acre vineyard in Sonoma Valley, California. He was drinking coffee after breakfast and on the phone with Ruben.

Stanley, as he was still called by his associates, was saying, "Tell me more about the nightclub, any problems?"

"No. None. Between four well-placed, simultaneous, powerful explosions and a roaring fire, it was annihilated. By the time the firemen and the police arrived it was already over."

"Excellent. I'm sure they've got policemen on their house now, and they're probably smart enough to move Miguel out of the city. You've already made a strong statement. This is a good time to slow down. In another day, move on to the policeman, Rafael. We can add the Spanish speaking employee, Maria, who if Erik's follow up info is as reliable as usual, worked at the bar and was their babysitter. If they have police on it, give their house a couple of days, then check it again."

"No problem. It's also possible to do the house while the policemen are standing by out front."

"Good. We've already sent a clear message, and eliminating the police detective will drive it home, unforgettably. The babysitter is the cherry on the dessert. I'll be talking to Alberto today, and let you know what I learn. Call me when you have your plan and your timing."

****

At precisely 10:00 a.m. the Macher had escorted General Mario Lopez into the safe house. Cash and Rafael had been waiting. Andre had been off trying to find Stanley's yacht and Johan, the captain of that yacht. Cash, the Macher and Rafael spent over an hour telling General Lopez what they'd learned about Stanley, the real estate developments and Alberto, his lawyer and overseer of the real estate developments.

General Lopez was tall, almost six feet and thin. He was close to sixty, and his hair was white. He wore an expensive blue suit, listened carefully, asked intelligent questions, and took notes. When they finished explaining what they knew—how the money always came into the Cayman Islands in untraceable shell corporations, then out to the developments in other shell corporations, so the investors were always untraceable—General Lopez stood, walked around slowly with his hands clasped behind his back. Eventually, he looked at all three of the men who'd been filling him in one by one, staring at their eyes. To all of them he finally said, "Yes, you were right to ask me to come. Now, how can we find more about them and the money in their real estate developments?"

Cash spoke up, "General, we'd like to propose that first, we call Alberto, Stanley's lawyer. We'd like you to alarm him, frighten him. You will know how to do that, but the general outline is to tell him that he's believed to be a collaborator in a three-hundred-and-fifty-million-dollar theft from the Venezuelan military. Tell him that you have former colleagues, who, at your request, are able to bring him back to stand trial in Venezuela. The only way he can prevent that is by helping us. That should get us a meeting today. To begin, we want to find Stanley, then we want to learn everything you know about the money. I'm going to turn this over to Itzac, the Macher, to describe how we plan to accomplish that."

The Macher turned to his friend, "Mario, here's what we know so far about the money: I'll do the math—it cost about six hundred thousand to build an average unit that costs eight hundred thousand. That means the maximum profit, without other costs is two hundred thousand. Including other costs, like buying the land, administrating and maintaining the development, sales costs, security, office staff, permits, taxes, etc. I'd guess that the total profit at about a hundred thousand per unit. If they'd built seventy units that means they'd make seven million.

They're still pouring in thirty million in future building, that is to say 50 more units, and that was just the one development. If my math is right, so far, they were twenty-three million in the red on one development. Let's multiply that by three and consider that one development would have 300 units or 180 more than the others. I calculated that after investing at least two hundred million, they're still a hundred and fifty million behind. He stood, then concluded, "If they had three hundred and fifty million, they were also likely to build at least two more developments. This is an estimate, but I'd guess their three hundred and fifty million will be under water for fifteen or twenty years."

The Macher watched General Lopez think this through. He decided to help his friend, "I'm imagining you're asking—why steal three hundred and fifty millionand piss it away for twenty years? Whoever is behind this will be dead before they make any real money." The Macher smiled. "Okay, so think about this carefully… First, you make the money disappear – which they obviously did extremely well. But then you don't want anyone to find it. What's better than hiding it in real estate developments for twenty years? Who would ever suspect that these cash poor, long-term developments are being funded with stolen money?"

The General nodded, a sparkle in his eyes, "I think I see where this is going. Suppose he'd like to see some more money sooner? What better way to help him accomplish that then offer to invest say fifty million in one of his developments? And what better way to learn more about exactly what they've done, their timing, and what they're doing now, then becoming their partner?"

The Macher nodded. "That's our idea. That's what we want to suggest."

Rafael, who'd been listening carefully, finally spoke up, "You're impressive, General."

"Thank you, but before we get ahead of ourselves, let's face the obvious difficult question. Where are we going to get this kind of money? I guarantee you that the Venezuelan Military is not going to throw good money after bad. And remember, if we're right about him, this Stanley won't even touch a Venezuelan partner."

"We've thought about this." The Macher touched his friend's shoulder. "I'm going to be the buyer. I can afford to put up the money in a trust account. I am actually a credible buyer—I can get several banks and other respected financial experts to vouch for me. I can get those things under another name I've used before for other private business, David Weinberg. My financial experts are used to using that name." The Macher nodded.

He went on, "My work as a diamond trader gives me a good reason to put some real money away safely in a long-term investment. Stanley doesn't know me, and if he checks me out, I'll pass easily as a reliable businessman and as a credible partner." He passed a file over to Cash. "Here's the information you'll need for David Weinberg."

Rafael spoke up, summarizing, "Okay, so here's where I think we are: First, we scare him, then we get whatever he knows about Stanley's whereabouts. At least how he gets in touch with him. Finally, we make him set up a meeting for a potential substantial investor, the Macher—aka David Weinberg."

Cash and the Macher nodded agreement simultaneously.

"Would you like me at that meeting?" Rafael asked. "It might be better if he doesn't see me hear about kidnapping him back to Venezuela. Though, so you know, I absolutely support your plan, and if I have to, I'll tell that to my captain or to anyone else that you need help with."

"That's enough for me." General Lopez said. "I'm going to call a Venezuelan friend and colleague, Colonel Daniel Bolivar, he's a leader in this investigation. He's in Venezuela, unlike me. He worked for me for years, and he's loyal. He'll stand by to help however he can. Let's call Alberto now."

****

At 1:00 p.m., General Lopez and Cash were seated in Alberto's conference room. Unsurprisingly, it turned out that the General was a formidable frightener. He simply told Alberto that his management and financial supervision of Stanley's three real estate developments indisputably made him a collaborator in a three-hundred-and fifty-million-dollar theft from the Venezuelan military. He went on to specify that there was a Venezuelan military Colonel, that he trusted, with a plane and four (DGCIM) military counterintelligence special forces crack operatives standing by to pick him up and bring him back. That in fact, if he called him now, Alberto would be in Venezuela this evening. Before Alberto could even digest that, Cash explained, unequivocally, that Stanley must never know about this meeting and our subsequent conversations, that Alberto's only possible way, his only chance, to avoid a Venezuelan court martial was to help us however he can. Alberto's face changed. Unable to suppress waves of anxiety, he looked like he was having a heart attack. He took a minute to stand, walk around, regain his composure. It wasn't working.

"Can we rely on you, unconditionally, Alberto?" General Lopez asked, purposefully.

"Yes sir, definitely… Yes, sir." Alberto repeated, then he nodded, convincingly. "Yes, yes, sir," he said, again and sat down.

"Good," the General replied. "Let's move on. Cash, can you please take the lead?"

"Yes, of course." Cash nodded, "Alberto, can you help us with how to locate Stanley—where he is, and how to contact him?"

"I'll tell you what I know." Alberto took another minute. When he began answering, it was apparent that he was trying to cooperate. "Okay, Stanley's gone, I don't know where… He's using another identity—he didn't tell me what it is… When he contacts me, I still call him Stanley and he's good with that… He uses multiple phones and changes the numbers regularly. He also makes calls and sends texts from his computer. He uses a VPN (virtual private network) to mask the identity and location of his IP address. He uses an app called Signal for security and encryption for his phones and his desktop. Using a combo of his VPN and Signal, he's able to keep communication open while masking his location. I have a number today that he'll only answer if I call it. That number won't work tomorrow. What I do know is that he has a PO box in Las Vegas where I can get a letter to him. That number won't change, and I'll give it to you. He has someone in Vegas who picks it up and forwards it someplace else, where I don't know." He wrote down the PO box number and gave it to Cash.

General Lopez took over. "That's helpful… Okay, here's the next important thing that we'd like you to do. We've reached out to a qualified, accomplished, investor," he described David Weinberg. "He's prepared to invest fifty million dollars in your largest development, the project that envisions 350 units. Our analysis suggests that Stanley could welcome a current, discrete, reliable investment of significant cash. We want you to arrange a meeting with Stanley—"

"Sorry to interrupt, sir, but I'm certain that Stanley won't personally take this meeting. He never meets new people. However, provided that Stanley is interested in this, which, I believe, you have reason to be hopeful about—a reputable influx of considerable cash could be well received. What I think I could try to do is arrange a meeting with his personal assistant, Erik Foster. Erik can quickly get an answer from Stanley."

"That's a start. Our investor, Mr. Weinberg, has travel plans, so he needs to move quickly. He will meet with his representative wherever he chooses tomorrow. We will provide you with all of the details about Mr. Weinberg, including references, investing history and financial statements. This offer won't last long if we can't work out specifics quickly."

"I'll call him as soon as you give me that information. I'll try to set this up tomorrow. Would you like to be here when I call him?"

Cash replied, "No. That's not necessary. I won't look over your shoulder, nor, in any way, get in your way during the call. But I would like you to record the call, then play it back for us." He took out a briefcase. "Here's the information on Mr. Weinberg that the General promised we'd provide." He gave David Weinberg's file to Alberto.

The General went on, "Please call him now. We'll wait outside and listen to the recording when you're finished."

****

Outside, Cash called Andre. "We've talked with Alberto. General Lopez was very convincing. In fact, I'm sure he changed Alberto's life. He's setting up a meeting with Stanley or one of his people with the Macher, a.k.a. David Weinberg, a potential investor, tomorrow."

Andre laughed, "You guys are bold, I'll give you that."

"Alberto would have made you a partner in his firm if the General had told him to… No, I'm not kidding. I discouraged that, because you'd make such a lousy lawyer… Sorry, buddy… Well, fuck you, too… He also gave us a PO box in Las Vegas where someone picks up Stanley's mail. It's our only lead to finding him. I'll give you the info… Yes, please go there right away. Find whoever picks up the mail and do what you do best to get him to tell you where Stanley lives now. While you're at it, Stanley has a new name and a new disguise—that's why you missed him at the airport hotel, though I'd wager that in your prime, that never would have happened… No, kiss your own ass… See what you can learn about his new name and his new disguise… Yes, I'm done bossing you around, for now… No, I spoke too soon —there is one more thing. What did you learn about the boat?... Yes, I'm sure you did a great job… It's out of commission for at least a week… Johan is staying at a hotel on Marcos Island?... You still do good work, even if you're insufferable… No, I'm not going back into therapy… I wasn't doing better then… And don't call me a pussy…"

*****

Back in Alberto's conference room, General Lopez and Cash heard the tape of Alberto's call with Stanley. He didn't use his new name, didn't reveal where he was living or what he was doing. Alberto replayed the most important part: "First, confirm that he has the money in his specified trust account. Then, scan me all of the references for this potential investor, David Weinberg. You can scan it to this phone number. It will only work for one hour. If I like—no, if I'm impressed by—what I see, he can meet with Erik tomorrow in Chicago. If he convinces Erik, we will do a more thorough background check. If he's deemed a trustworthy, desirable investor, we'll talk further. Truthfully, I have to say that this could interest me. New money will be helpful, both for cash flow and for our presentation to others. What is your opinion?"

"He was presented, then recommended, as a legitimate, reliable investor. He's older, over eighty, and a very successful diamond trader over many, many years. He's made a fortune. It's easy to understand why, at his age, he'd want to park a large chunk of this money safely. As you'll see when you read what he's sent, he's very highly thought of by his bankers and other serious financial people. I think he's potentially a discrete, unobtrusive junior partner."

"That's a good recommendation and helpful. I'll call you within an hour with my decision." Stanley signed off.

The General spoke to Alberto, "You handled this well. It will be in your favor when I speak with my colleague, the Colonel."

"Thank you," Alberto replied.

The General added, "When he calls back, tell him that we'll meet him at the Drake Hotel in Chicago. I'll book a suite for tonight."

"Good, I'll follow up." Alberto said. "Thank you both." Alberto nodded, and they left his office.

****

Back at the safe house, Cash and the General filled the Macher in on all of it. When they were done, the Macher nodded, then simply said, "Well done. This all sounds doable."

"Good," the General replied, "Let's work out the details…"

The Macher thought about where to start, "Okay, General, how would you like to handle this at the hotel?"

"I don't want him to see me, but suppose I lock myself in the bedroom, and set it up so I can watch the meeting via hidden cameras set up in the room where you're meeting. I can conceal the cameras, set them up and watch the meeting live on my computer."

"I'll help you get the cameras today," The Macher volunteered. "I can also help you set them up where they won't be visible."

"Thank you. Let's set the meeting at ten a.m. tomorrow morning, and let's get to Chicago tonight," the General suggested.

"Good," Itzac agreed, "I'll also book a separate room for you."

Cash jumped in. "You don't need me for this. If you concur, I'll call Alberto and find a time to talk further. I have an idea I'd like to discuss with him."

Cash left the Macher and the General sitting around the island in the kitchen, then went into the living room, sat on the couch and called Alberto.

When he got him, Cash explained, "I'd like to talk further, just the two of us. I have an idea I'd like to discuss with you."

Alberto replied, "As I hope I've demonstrated, I heard General Lopez, and I understood the importance and the consequences of what he presented."

"That's been noted, counselor."

"Good. What's a good time to discuss further with you?"

"Let's talk once I finish with Mr. Weinberg and the General today. That will be this afternoon, after they go to Chicago."

"I'll make myself available. How's three p.m.?"

"Fine."

After Cash hung up, the Macher spoke up. "Have at it. I know where you're going. We'll give you a report from Chicago tomorrow."

****

At 3:00 p.m., Cash was back in Alberto's office, this time he was facing him across his desk. Cash dove right in, "I'm guessing that you know quite a lot about the banking arrangements for the real estate developments. More specifically, my first question then is does Stanley get distributions from the real estate holdings to a personal bank account?"

"He does."

"Do you make these distributions and, if so, where do you deposit them?"

"I make them twice a year to his own account that was created in our Cayman Islands bank. The account is not in his name. It's numbered and he's able, via a regularly changing code, to withdraw money from it."

"How much money would you guess is usually in that account?"

"With the twice-a-year deposits, on average there must be close to a million dollars."

"I'm guessing that he takes out his spending money from that account."

"I don't see the statements, but I'm sure he does."

"If I'm right, I'm wondering if, with the General's help and the help of his friend, the Colonel, and perhaps even a Miami police detective who's working with us, we can put a hold on that account and freeze it."

"That's complicated, but not impossible. To accomplish this, I believe it would be wise to go to the Cayman Islands, with most importantly the General and the Colonel. They can begin by talking with the person I work with. He, in turn, will give you the right person in compliance to discuss it further."

"That makes sense."

"I don't need to tell you how Stanley would feel about that."

"That's the idea. After the General and Mr. Weinberg have their meeting tomorrow, let's plan a trip to the Cayman Islands."

****

Cash was back at the South Beach safe house when he heard from Callie.

"Hey babe, missing you," she said, warmly.

"Likewise."

"How did it go with the General?"

"He's a pro and a very smart, good guy on top of that. It took him about two minutes to convince Alberto to do exactly what he wanted. The Macher told me a little bit about the General. He went into exile after the current president, a dictator, stole the election. After he left, there were scandalous lies, rumors that he'd participated in stealing the money. He was never officially accused, but nothing would please him more than proving that the false accusations were a lie."

"If he finds and returns their three hundred and fifty million dollars, it can only help."

"Yes, you're right, but truthfully, I'm worried about all of this. Stanley already has another identity. He looks different, and he's living somewhere else, we have no idea where. Alberto gave us a PO box in Las Vegas, but that's all we have. Andre is there, waiting for someone to pick up his mail. That could take weeks, and, in all likelihood, he'll deliver it to yet another PO box., and we'll still have no idea where he lives. The guy has fooled the entire Venezuelan government and military, and he's got crackerjack killers after all of us. He's formidable, he's unpredictable, he has no scruples, and he's ahead of us...What they did to Alvaro's nightclub is just the beginning..."

"Alvaro and Sara are both very upset about that."

"I'm sure... I'm worried about what comes next..."

"Understandably, especially if he's ahead of us and so able."

"He's going to start killing people soon. It's who he is."

"You're scaring me."

"You have reason to be frightened. Remember Luis, and the photographer... Let's hope the General finds something in Chicago, something that will allow us to play offense."

"Well, I'm sorry to have to say this, but I'll certainly feel better when you're doing that. It's when you're at your best, and I know you'll worry less."

"You're right, and thank you for that, my darling. How are Sara and Alvaro doing?"

"As I'm sure you can imagine, they're very upset about losing the Midnight Mirage."

"Yes, I do understand that… But are they okay otherwise?"

"Yes, as you know, they're resilient… They love being in Cuba. It's where they really fell in love, and it has special meaning for them. And not surprisingly, they're just great with Young Cash, so very happy with him. They love being here with him. They walk all over the city, the three of them. I wouldn't be at all surprised if they move here… Can I change the subject?"

"Of course."

"Babe, I want to come back. It's not that there's anything wrong here, it's just that I want to be with you. If I'm there, I'll be able to help… and I don't need to tell you that this idea of 'keeping the women safe' is just plain macho, sexist bullshit."

"Wanting to keep you safe is also part of loving you."

"I repeat—Macho, sexist bullshit."

"OK. Right. Can we agree to disagree?... Never mind… Truthfully, I'd love to see you, and I have an idea. I'm hoping we'll be going to the Cayman Islands very soon to freeze Stanley's money. Why don't we meet there—I'm guessing we could meet in two days—and after, you can come back with me wherever that turns out to be."

"I'd love that."

"Me too. I'll let you know as soon as I know anything… Talk soon."

"Ciao, baby doll. You cheered me right up."

****

The General and his friend, Itzac, the Macher, a.k.a. David Weinberg, arrived at the Drake Hotel at 8:30 p.m. It was situated wonderfully on Lake Michigan, set at the northern starting point of Michigan Avenue's glamorous Gold Coast. Their suite was ten floors up, and it had a lovely view of the lake. It didn't take them long to set up the cameras—well hidden, so they couldn't be seen. When they were done, they enjoyed drinks and dinner downstairs in the Coq d'Or, a Gold

Coast neighborhood favorite. The legendary bar opened on December 6th, 1933, just after the repeal of prohibition.

Now, it was the following morning, 9:45 a.m., and they were set up as they'd planned in the suite—the General was hidden in the locked bedroom. The Macher sat comfortably on a chair in the living room. At 10:00 a.m., precisely, Erik knocked on the door.

****

At that same time, Cash got a call in his South Beach safe house. It was Andre. "A pretty, young woman, maybe thirty-five, picked up his mail. I followed her to her car and braced her."

"Did you beat up a young woman, Andre?"

"I don't know why I even help you out. Every step of the way you make unbelievable accusations, insult me, and finally, misinterpret and get the outcome wrong."

"OK, sorry, I can't resist. So just tell me what happened."

"I showed her my own persuasive police badge, then she told me exactly what she does. No problem. In truth, she has no idea what she actually does. She certainly doesn't know Stanley nor heard of his other name, Brendan. She was hired by his assistant, and she believes she forwards occasional letters to his mail order business which moved from Las Vegas to a new address."

"And?"

"She sends it to a PO box in San Francisco. Here's the number." Andre texted it. "She doesn't know anything else."

"Are you certain?"

"You are dumb as dirt. I made a dinner date with her. Do you think she'd go out with me if she was holding back?"

"You're having dinner with her? Are you crazy?"

"It's not tonight. I'm on my way to San Francisco, to find out where the mail is going. I'll see the lovely young woman after I come back."

"You're unbelievable, lover boy… Well, at least you knew to follow the mail."

"What you are is a thankless douche bag…You're lucky I even call you." Andre hung up.

****

General Lopez was watching Erik Foster questioning David Weinberg's bank, financial and personal references. So far, it had gone very well. Itzac's references were, in fact, excellent. People seemed to like doing business with him, and unquestionably, they genuinely liked him. So, what was bothering the General? He wasn't sure. Erik was smart, articulate, undeniably a well-mannered gentleman. General Lopez stared at him on his computer. He watched his way of talking, the way he gestured, gracefully with his hands. Then, just like that, he got it. He knew this man from years ago. Yes, he'd met him, though he couldn't say how. The General took several photos of Erik on the computer via his screen grab tool, then he went into the bathroom, closed the door and called Colonel Bolivar's office in Venezuela. When he reached his colleague, the Colonel, he sent him the picture from his computer.

"I know this man, Colonel. I want you to run this picture through our data base—put our best technical extra on it. Have him cross check, adjust the picture, use every trick he knows—just find out who this man is. He goes by Erik Foster, but I'm sure that's not his real name. He speaks fluent English and passes as a California style American. I think he could be Venezuelan. Go back ten years. I want his real name, his work history and what he did. I'm especially curious about when he left Venezuela. This is the highest possible priority. Please call me anytime, as soon as you know anything."

****

Cash called Rafael, he wanted to meet him, bring him up to date, get his help in finding Stanley who now went by the name Brendan, and convince him to come with him to the Cayman Islands. A woman answered his phone at the police station. She abruptly told Cash to hold on.

In less than a minute, another man came on, "Who's calling Detective Rafael?"

"Who is this?" Cash asked. "And why do you want to know?"

"This is his Captain. Again, who is this?"

"This is his friend, Cash Logan. We're working together, Captain. My son-in-law, Alvaro, was related to Luis, who was Rafael's friend. Alvaro was kidnapped from Rafael's car in the police parking lot. Luis was killed. I need to talk with Detective Rafael."

"You can't. He was killed this morning, shot dead leaving his apartment an hour ago."

"Damnit! I'm so sorry… Damnit, damnit, how can I help?"

"Any idea who did this?"

"Yes, and please record my statement, because I can't come in today."

"Okay, this is being recorded."

"Captain, I can't prove any of this, but I'd bet that he was killed by a Venezuelan special forces' operative. All I know is that his first name is Ruben. He's one of two from the Venezuelan General Directorate of Military Counterintelligence, and he works now for Stanley White. Stanley now goes by a new name, and we have no idea where he is. That's one of the things I wanted to talk with Rafael about. I believe his killer is one of the men who killed Luis, and Garcia, an informant working for me. He also beat up my daughter and burned down my son-in-law's nightclub, the Midnight Mirage. That happened the night before last."

"Yes, I know about that."

"Killing Rafael is another message to those of us trying to bring down Stanley… I was hoping that Rafael would come with us to the Cayman Islands to help freeze one of Stanley's bank accounts."

"Can you do it without him? Do you need someone else?"

"No, I don't think we'll need another policeman. General Lopez is coming, and he's bringing the Venezuelan Colonel who's one of the principal people heading up the investigation about the missing money. They're prepared to tell the bank that they want to freeze the assets in the account pending an international criminal investigation. That should be enough."

"Yes."

"I'll miss Rafael…he was a good man."

"The best…please let me know what you're doing."

"I'm working on all of this. As soon as I know more, I'll call you."

"Normally, I'd bring you in now, but Rafael told me about you. You're *Pulp Fiction,* aren't you?"

"Not literally, but that's what he called me."

"He trusted you, and that had to be earned. Please just call me when you can. My name is Jim Holden. Here's my private number." He gave the number to Cash.

"I will and thank you for giving me a little time. I need to tell everyone who's working on this with me what happened. Again, I'm so sorry."

"We all are. He's irreplaceable. I'll wait to hear from you." Captain Holden hung up.

Cash looked at his phone. He had a call from the Macher and the General from Chicago.

He called the Macher right back. "Bad news," he said, right off. "Put the General on too, I want to tell you before you report on your meeting."

"We're on the speaker," the Macher said.

"Can you hear me?" General Lopez asked.

"I can," Cash answered. "There's no easy way to tell this, but Detective Rafael was shot and killed this morning."

"Shit," the Macher said. "I'm assuming it was Stanley's killer."

"Yes, so am I. This took me by surprise. He's so damn fast…"

"Yes. Rafael was such a good man… Let's come back to this… We have some better news, let me turn this over to Mario to fill you in, then we can come back."

The General started right in, "First off, Itzac was masterful. Erik was completely won over… He promised to get back to him in three days… But here's the other news. I was watching on the computer, and it took me several minutes, but I realized that I recognized Erik, Stanley's representative, from years ago. I called my Venezuelan colleague, Colonel Bolivar, right away, and I sent him a photo I took on my computer. I just heard back from him. Our technical guy worked his magic tricks and located him in our data base. Eight or nine years ago, Erik went by Raul. He was a messenger, an errand boy, and eventually an assistant on General Gabriel's staff. Soon after General Gabriel died, Raul left the Venezuelan military. No one knows where he went. His connection to General Gabriel, the mastermind behind the stolen three hundred and fifty million dollars, is enough for me to go all in. The murder this morning just makes it more urgent. Let's start by leaning on the Cayman Island bank to freeze Stanley's account."

"Are you prepared to make the case that the bank needs to freeze the assets in this account pending an investigation of criminal activity."

"Yes, I can make a convincing case that it's in the bank's interest to freeze the assets. But, as you know, I'm not an active general and I'm not living in Venezuela. So, as we discussed, for this important meeting, my friend, Colonel Bolivar, is joining us. He's directing this investigation and will speak authoritatively about this. The last thing any compliance officer needs is for the bank to be implicated in what might turn out to be a major international crime."

"Good. I'll call Alberto right away. You can meet his contact at the bank tomorrow afternoon."

The Macher spoke up, "I'd like to go back to Rafael. How can we stop this killer? What's his name?"

"I heard Stanley yell at him on the phone. He called him Ruben."

"I think Ruben will keep burning down property and killing people until we stop him."

Cash nodded. "I agree. Let me talk with Alberto about him, too. Let's speed all of this up. Can you call Andre, lean on him to use his resourcefulness to get an address in San Francisco quickly?"

"I can, and after losing Rafael, he'll do anything he can."

"I'll pursue both the Cayman Islands and finding Ruben with Alberto. I'll call him right away, then I'll call Callie. I'll tell her about Rafael, have her skip the Cayman Islands, then meet me back in Miami. She can help us with everything, especially after Stanley learns that we've frozen his bank account. I'll also talk with Sara and Alvaro about Rafael. They need to be extra careful now. Ruben or one of Stanley's other men is likely to go after them in Cuba."

****

Cash didn't waste any time with Alberto. "We need a meeting with your preferred banking officer in your Cayman Island bank, tomorrow."

"I'll set that up. I'll also give him a heads up that he'll need to have a compliance department officer standing by."

"Yes, General Lopez, and his colleague, Colonel Bolivar, who's one of the people in charge of the investigation of the stolen money, will be at the meeting. They won't leave until the bank account is frozen."

"You understand that the moment Stanley learns about that, I'm in danger."

"Yes, I've thought about that. What are you thinking?"

"I'm thinking I have to call him right after your meeting. I'll tell him something about how the General is very powerful and out of control. He and his associates took over on the bank account and applied the muscle of the Venezuelan military without my involvement. I'll tell him that I just learned about this from our banker. I'll also tell him that I understand that this is a serious setback for him. I'll then ask him what I can do to make up for this. If I'm right, he'll have something difficult, dangerous and important to him. I'll agree to it, and I'll let you know what it is."

"Be very careful."

"I'm very careful with him even when I'm not in trouble."

"I need another favor… Our friend, Detective Rafael, was killed this morning. I'm thinking Stanley man's Ruben did this. Is that likely?"

"Almost certain. From what little I know, he's the only one of his people that Stanley left behind."

"From what I've seen, he's a stone-cold killer, relentless."

"I don't know. I've never met him."

"Can you find out where he is? We need to stop him."

"Not now. I can't even ask Stanley about this, if I'm telling him that his bank account is being frozen. He will be furious with me. You'll have to wait until he calms down and hope I can come to some kind of resolution with him."

"Alright, I understand. For all of us, I hope you can do that."

"I'll talk with him after I hear from you, and I'll let you know."

CHAPTER FOUR

General Lopez and Colonel Bolivar arrived in the Cayman Islands that evening. By 10:00 a.m. the next morning, they were in Mr. Charles Burke's office, accompanied by one of his associates, sitting at a round conference table. Mr. Burke was the officer in charge of all of Alberto's accounts with the bank.

The General began, "My name is General Lopez. I was a senior military officer with the Venezuelan government. I've brought my former colleague, Colonel Bolivar, who's investigating hundreds of millions of dollars that have been stolen from the Venezuelan military, to express our concerns. I'm going to turn this over to him.

The Colonel stood. He was tall and distinguished looking. His manner was authoritative. "We have reason to believe that significant amounts of these stolen monies have been deposited in, then moved through, your bank. The methodology of these deposits, the use of shell corporations, make them untraceable. It goes without saying that this is an international criminal act. We're requesting that you freeze this account, pending an investigation." The General showed him a piece of paper with the number of Stanley's personal account.

Mr. Burke nodded, "I was prepared for this meeting by Counselor Alberto Leon. He told me about General Lopez, and specifically described you, why he included you, and about your concerns. He also explained your position, your status. As such, I've asked one of our senior compliance officers to sit in." He introduced Mr. Christopher Whittaker.

"Of course," the Colonel replied. After a beat, he bluntly asked, "Is it worse to irritate an important client or to be implicated in what certainly will turn out to be a major international crime?"

After that, it took less than ten minutes to convince these men to freeze the account.

****

Half an hour later, Alberto was waiting at the phone when Stanley called him back. "Why did you call me?" Stanley asked.

"I just got bad news, and I wanted to tell you right away."

"What?"

"I just heard from Charles Burke, our officer at the Cayman Island bank. He's been contacted by a Venezuelan General, General Mario Lopez, who included Colonel Bolivar, a Venezuelan military officer investigating the stolen money, three hundred and fifty million dollars, that went missing five years ago, in their meeting."

"General Lopez, I've heard that name. How could they possibly get to this bank?"

"I don't know. The General is out of control, and the Colonel is very powerful. Colonel Bolivar applied the muscle of the Venezuelan military without my involvement. He must have uncovered something in Venezuela, and now he wants to freeze your account while they investigate international criminal activity. I can't stop him, and I can't stop the bank from worrying about being implicated in a major international crime."

"This changes everything. You are to blame. You chose this bank, you chose the banker, Mr. Burke, to work with you, and now, you may be responsible for shutting off my source of funds."

"I understand that this is a serious setback… I'd like to help however I can. Is there anything I can do to make it up to you?"

"I can't tolerate even speaking with you now. It's all I can do not to have you killed. I need to think." Stanley White a.k.a. Brendan Dubois hung up.

****

Cash was thinking about Alberto when Andre called.

Andre started right in, "Bad news. I'm actually at the San Francisco post office which was supposed to get Stanley's mail. The PO box is closed, no forwarding address. This is a dead end."

"You sure you're at the right post office?"

"My old friend, who's gotten dumb as dirt, is at it again. Of course I'm at the right post office. I showed the man at the desk my badge, asked him for whatever was in the PO box. He said he couldn't give me what was in a PO box without a warrant. Always ready, I supplied him with a warrant that I'd written up last night. He explained that he still couldn't give me what was in the box, only his supervisor could do that, but he could confirm its status. I said let's start with that. He looked it up and smugly announced that it had been closed. I talked to the supervisor, and he confirmed that it had been closed this morning, no forwarding address, no phone, nothing. As I said, this, at least, is a dead end."

"They're fast. Alberto just let Stanley know that they were freezing his bank account. He recognized General Lopez's name. In any event, he's closing off all access."

"Any other ideas?"

"Not yet. Just a question. Did the person who closed the PO box leave a name?"

"The man who opened and closed the PO box said his name was James Olsen. I'd bet that it's a fake name."

"You think? Maybe his parents named him from the Superman comic?"

"What?"

"Jimmy Olsen, the photojournalist for *The Daily Planet...*"

"How can Callie stand you?" Andre hung up.

****

Stanley a.k.a. Brendan was on his patio overlooking his expansive vineyard. He was drinking a fine red, a Cabernet Sauvignon, harvested, pressed, fermented, clarified, aged and bottled right here on his own property, grapes carefully, painstakingly, grown in his vineyard. He loved the dark fruit flavors of black cherry, blackcurrant (cassis) and blackberry. He could taste the aroma of vanilla and clove (from aging in an oak barrel). It always made him feel better, distracted him from unpleasant things, to enjoy his own wine. After another sip, he set down his wine glass, looked out over the vineyard.

He had been thinking about what to do. Alberto had worried him, more than he let on. The Venezuelan military new too much, and after making several calls to trusted high-level Venezuelan friends, including a trusted advisor to the president, he knew that General Mario Lopez was still a dangerous adversary, and the man he'd brought in, Colonel Bolivar, was well connected, a capable, powerful ally. He had no idea how the General was brought in, or how much he actually knew, but the damage was done. He'd always known that this could happen, he'd never thought, however, that it would happen so unexpectedly.

He'd underestimated this odd group around Cash Logan. They'd secretly taken a photo of him, they'd blown up his yacht, they'd interested the Miami police in his business, and, he was certain, they'd somehow brought General Lopez into the picture. He'd had Erik and Tim check them out early on, after the incident with the photo. All they'd learned is that his son-in-law, Alvaro, was related to Luis, the journalist that acquired the photo and was subsequently eliminated by Ruben. They'd also learned that the so-called "Cash" was an international trader who was connected to a well-known diamond trader, a former mercenary military strategist, and other unlikely people as far off as Cuba. Inexplicably, he was married to a restaurateur in Seattle. All of this didn't create any kind of clear picture, and it had led nowhere. There was no evidence that these people were as capable as they turned out to be. Still, the damage had been done. His bank account had been frozen, a Miami police detective, a well-positioned Venezuelan Colonel and a retired Venezuelan General had begun investigating him, and it was just a matter of time before they subpoenaed him, and then, in court, they demanded the origins of the money from the real estate developments.

After revisiting all of this, Stanley had come to a definite, albeit difficult conclusion—it was time to sell all the real estate, get out, disappear, period, even at a substantial loss, and he had to do this ASAP. He didn't need $350,000,000 any time soon. Many real estate developers had expressed serious interest—several had made respectable offers—in his three advanced projects, and the other two properties in early phases of development, and now he had to sell discretely and very quickly. The obvious man to do this was Alberto, who knew the developments and who'd fielded the various offers that had come in. He could be made to understand that his life depended on doing this secretly and exactly as he was instructed. Whatever else he may have done, Stanley knew that he could bring Alberto reliably back into the fold by threatening his life, unmistakably, and promising great wealth, equally unfailingly. Stanley entered a new phone number into his security system, then called Alberto.

"You've betrayed me… I'm sure you're in contact with Cash Logan and General Lopez," Stanley started right in.

"No, I called you as soon as I knew anything, and I stand ready to help."

"You're unfaithful, possibly a traitor. Understanding that, I've thought through some very important work for you which could give you a second chance, a chance to live… The most important condition is that you can't tell anything to Cash Logan or to the General. Can I rely on you, absolutely? Think carefully before you answer this question, because if I even suspect you don't keep your word, I will have you killed instantly."

"Yes, sir. You can rely on me… I do understand."

"Now then, just listen carefully, everything I'm going to propose is non-negotiable, and your life depends on accomplishing it precisely as directed… I want you to sell all three of the real estate developments and both of the projects in early development—quickly and quietly. I'm prepared to take a loss, I'm prepared to delay some portion of the payments, but I must walk away quickly with fifty to seventy-five million dollars. Time is of the essence. You already know multiple potential buyers. Choose the most financially able, the most discrete, the most reliable. They must be able to do this very quickly and privately. If you accomplish this as I've asked, I'll give you one percent of the immediate money—that should be five hundred thousand, minimum, and one and a half percent of the money coming in later, that could be five million. I will guarantee the money coming in later by creating a trust to receive it in the closing documents. This trust will hold the money, and you'll control the trust. I want your answer right now. I also want your absolute understanding that any deviation from my instructions, any communication of any of this information to anyone, will bring certain death, you will be killed at once. You have just minutes to give me your answer and express your confirmation of your understanding of my conditions."

In less than twenty seconds, Alberto said, "I will sell the real estate, and I do understand and accept your conditions." Alberto smiled, evidently pleased.

"Very well. Let's begin the specifics immediately. First, I'd like you to convey a message to Cash Logan and General Lopez, our unexpected, formidable adversaries, and through them, whoever they've involved in the local police department. Let's propose to these men that we make a deal, a way to co-exist. I have an idea that should interest them—we need to buy time to complete this sale privately. My proposal should give us several days. Once this sale is done, I plan to bring our communication with these people to an abrupt end.

****

When Cash came back to his safe house with General Lopez, he had a message from Alberto. Before he called him back, the phone rang. Cash answered, "Hello, this is—"

Before he could get out another word, he was interrupted, "Captain Jim Holden here. More bad news. Alvaro and your daughter's house just exploded and caught fire. It was a serious professional job, and the house is destroyed. Though the firemen just arrived, they say the fire is unstoppable, and the house will surely burn down."

"Agh! I'm putting you on the speaker. General Lopez, who I told you about, is here working with me."

"Fine."

"What the hell happened? I thought you had policemen watching the house?"

"Yes, we left one man on. As best we figured, someone broke into the house late last night unseen. Let's assume it's the same guy you suspected, Ruben. He must have set the bombs and the incendiary devices on timers, then left unnoticed. It's four p.m. now. The explosions went off less than an hour ago."

"I'm guessing that there's no point to go to the house now."

"It's too late. You can come or send someone to walk through when the fire is out."

"This guy is too dangerous, and this is out of control."

"Yes. We need to stop him, right away."

"Give me half an hour to get organized. I need to call everyone, including Stanley's lawyer, Alberto. I'll also tell everyone involved, wherever they are, to get to a safe place, get protection if they need to. Damnit, they're too far ahead of us. I need to catch up, even get ahead. I'll call you back when I know more. Thanks for calling."

"You've got half an hour."

General Lopez interjected, "This is General Lopez, Captain. I'd like to find a time to talk with you, let you know what we're thinking."

"Are you sure that's wise?"

"I'll be careful. I know not to tell you anything you won't want to hear."

"I'll see you whenever you're ready."

"Thank you. I'll call you later today." He signaled Cash to turn off the phone.

"Are you sure you want to do that?" Cash asked the General.

"It's time. This is about to escalate. I'd like his help to clear the way."

"Okay, I get that. Now, I need to call everyone involved to let them know. Then let's call Alberto back, see where Stanley is and make a plan."

****

Cash called Sara, "Babe, please put this on speaker, I'd like Alvaro on this call…"

"Okay, he's on."

"Sorry, but I have more bad news. They blew up your house and burned it down less than an hour ago."

"Oh, no! No! No! No!" Sara started crying, uncontrollably.

Alvaro said, softly, "Give me a minute, I'll call you back."

"I'll wait by the phone."

Alvaro consoled Sara, then when her crying was under control, he called back. "I'm back," he said to Cash. "As hard as it is, we knew this was possible. Now, tell us how we can stop this?"

"We're working on that. The General just came back from the Cayman Islands, and they agreed to freeze Stanley's bank account. That's going to make him crazy. The General is here with me, and he's convinced that we're right about Stanley and the real estate. He's all in. He and the Macher met with one of Stanley's representatives. The Macher was posing as an interested investor. The Macher is scheduled to meet with this man again in three days. General Lopez, recognized the man from the past—he was somehow connected to General Gabriel Castillo, the man who stole the money before he died. General Lopez is getting help from Venezuela. We'll be talking to Alberto, who's talked to Stanley, as soon as we get off the phone. Depending on what he says, we're ready to play offense. We'll keep you both posted, and let you know if we need your help."

"I can come now and walk through the house."

"No, there's nothing left to do. I can do that for you, later… Sara, I know you're upset, this is what we worked so hard to avoid, but please stay focused and positive, we're going to manage this, and before it's over, I'm sure we'll need you. In the meantime, both of you, please take every precaution. Until we get ahead of this you're still in danger. It goes without saying that this is even more important for your son, my grandson."

"Not to worry," Sara said. "I'll be there, or as Callie might want to say it, I'll 'Just fucking man up!' You can count on us."

"Yes, of course," Alvaro added.

"I need to talk with Callie. I assume she's on her way here. Do you have her timing?"

Sara looked at her phone. "Her flight should arrive in about half an hour. An aside, only Callie would want to join you, actually step into this mess. You're a lucky husband."

"And a lucky dad."

"Thank you, dad, you know to reach me if you need me."

"I do. Thanks… Kiss my grandson, love to the three of you. I'll call you when I know more."

The General smiled at Cash. "You have a lovely family. Your wife reminds me of my own wife."

"Thank you, we should have a drink and share stories about these fine women when this is over. In the meantime, we all appreciate your help."

****

Alberto was sitting alone in his office, waiting for Cash's call. Since signing on with Stanley, this call, this relationship, had become complicated. He'd carefully thought about his decision, and he knew he'd done the right thing—both because Stanley was capable of having him killed if he hadn't, and because there was so much money for him in this that he could finally do what he'd always dreamed of. He privately longed to disappear into a life of luxury. And he knew the remote, exotic place where he wanted to go.

To accomplish this, what he had to do was to sell the real estate exactly as Stanley wanted, collect the initial money as Stanley had offered. He had already placed several calls, and at present, he had two serious buyers in hand. He had also been thinking about how to set this up so that he could get his share of the long-term money more quickly. He had an idea that would allow him to get the first monies to come in. As the lawyer, he could write the trust documents so that—inconspicuously—he would be in the first position. If he did this as he imagined, this detail would be hidden away, obfuscated by legal minutiae. It didn't work, however, unless he could keep Stanley from killing him before he got the money and left. To do this, he had to convince Stanley that he was absolutely his man, that he wasn't having side conversations with Cash—which is precisely what he was about to do, now.

At the same time, he had to fool Cash until he disappeared. Fooling Cash had to start right now on this call. Just as important, he had to convince General Lopez that he was still on his and Cash's team. He believed the General was capable of having his man send him back to Venezuela to face criminal charges if he ever suspected his duplicity. Long story short, this call was very important. His cell phone signaled a call, Cash. He picked it up.

"Thanks for calling, we have a lot to discuss."

"Before you tell me about your conversation, I want you to know that your fucking client had Ruben blow up and burn down my daughter and son-in-law's house."

"Yes, he told me that this step was imminent, and I can tell you that he was pleased to have sent that message."

"Well, you can tell him that freezing his bank account is just the beginning of what we intend to do. Next, we will—"

Alberto interrupted, "Excuse me, but please, let me reset this call. First, let's go back… My call with Stanley went relatively well. As I'd hoped in our—that is to say you and my—call, he did accept my explanation, and then, he wanted me to send another message for you."

"OK, what is it?"

"At the outset, he wants me to tell you how very unhappy he was with the unapproved photo that was taken of him, the way you attacked and damaged his boat, how you included a Miami police detective in your suspicions, your investigations, how you brought a Venezuelan General into your already distressed, adversary situation, and most recently, what you've done to freeze his bank account. He understands now that you're very capable and more than just a nuisance. He would like to make a deal with you, a way to co-exist that would work for both of you. He has some specific suggestions."

"Such as."

"He's agreed to meet with both of you, here in Florida, as soon as he's able to travel safely. He's had Covid, which he caught recently on an airplane, in spite of having every vaccination possible. He should be fit to travel in four or five days. He can also meet you in San Francisco perhaps a day earlier, if you'd prefer. I don't know what he's going to propose to you, but I know it's rare for him to meet anyone in person—I've only met him once myself. I also know that he wouldn't suggest a meeting unless he had something important to offer, something that would definitely interest you. He did say to tell you that he's had several investors that could be moving Venezuelan military monies. He'll give you more details when you meet. In the meantime, he'll give you the specifics of the location of the bank accounts where this money came from. I can personally assure you that he would never suggest anything like this if he didn't want to make an accommodation. He'd like to plan this meeting as soon as possible. He will meet you Saturday, that's five days from now, in San Francisco or on Sunday in Florida. Will you agree to this meeting?"

"Perhaps," General Lopez replied. "Cash?" He looked at Cash.

Cash spoke up, "I don't know. We won't even consider it until he calls off his destroyer, his killer, Ruben. He'll have to convince us that he'll leave us alone, that he's out of the picture, before we respond to his suggestion."

"I can convey that to him. I'm fairly sure that he'll pull Ruben back."

"That's not enough. We want proof that this maniac won't touch any of our people, or their property, or their friends, anywhere. That includes those who are out of the country."

"Today, I can ask. I can make it a non-negotiable precondition for any further communication."

"Do that and then we'll talk further."

****

Stanley was still on his patio. He had Tim, Carlos and Erik with him. Erik had just returned from his meeting with the Macher in Chicago.

Before Erik could give his report, Stanley said, "We'll have to put the new investor on hold. The landscape has changed dramatically, and I want to let you know where we are… I've decided to sell all of the real estate investments, privately and quickly. Alberto is discretely managing this. As *The Godfather* explained it—I made him an offer he couldn't refuse… The deal should be done in three or four days. I'll explain more about that later but suffice it to say that we'll be going into the next phase. To do that, I'll need some time to finalize working out specific next steps. In the meantime, let's bring back Johan. I have another job for Ruben, and we'll have him meet us later.

The phone rang. It was a code, and Stanley knew that Alberto was calling. He turned to the others, "Alberto is calling. Tim, can you give me your phone, and I'll call him back?" A minute later he had Alberto on the line.

"Yes, you can tell them I will take responsibility for withdrawing Ruben provided that they agree to a meeting in five or six days… You can promise them that I have another job for Ruben until this is over… We'll give them a date tomorrow… You've already contacted four capable buyers. That's excellent… I'll call you later to discuss details… Yes, you can take charge of the documents... Lawyers working for you would be best… We'll want close to eighty to eighty-five percent of our estimate of full value, over time… The reduction is a bonus for speed, privacy, acceptability and reliability of scheduling future payments… Once we've agreed on a schedule, I'll take charge of choosing several banks other than the Cayman Islands… I'll call you within an hour to follow up…"

Alberto replied, "Sir, I just wanted to say that I appreciate this great opportunity, and you can rely on me to meet your specific conditions."

"That's good to know. There's one more thing… I'm trusting you Alberto, but to assure your loyalty, I'm going to have Ruben stay with you, live with you, listen in on your calls, your meetings, be at your side, at all times, until the deal is done… As such, you can reassure Cash that in fact, you will be watching Ruben, that he'll be under your supervision, every moment… I'll personally guarantee that his full-time job until after our meetings will be confirming your loyalty…. No, that too, is non-negotiable…"

Alberto had turned red. He was sweating when Stanley hung up.

****

Cash and General Lopez, who'd asked Cash to call him Mario, were sitting at the counter in the safe house with Callie, who'd arrived just half an hour earlier. They'd been bringing her up to date. She'd been listening, carefully, in her thoughtful way, missing nothing. When they finished telling her about Alberto's last call, she asked the obvious question, "Why would Stanley, whatever his name is, want to make a deal with us? More specifically, why does he think he *can* make a deal with us?"

"We've been asking the same question." Cash nodded. "I'm sure he's worried that his bank account is frozen, worried about Mario's Venezuelan investigation into his business and financial affairs, but he can't possibly think that we'd make any kind of deal that would stop any of that?"

"Maybe he knows that and maybe he wants the meeting to buy some time," the General wondered. "Maybe he needs time to rethink, to come up with something else, an overwhelming threat, something he believes will make us back off?"

"What might that be?" Callie asked.

"We don't know." Cash said.

The phone rang, Cash saw that it was Alberto. "Let's take that, see if Alberto can shed some light on this?" Cash took the call. "Alberto, I'm here with General Lopez and Callie, my wife. I'm putting you on the speaker." He did. "We're confused. Even if he's agreed to call Ruben off, and we agree to meet with him, we don't understand what kind of deal is possible."

"Let me take one question at a time. First, he's sending Ruben to keep an eye on me. He doesn't fully trust me and he wants Ruben to come live with me, observe me, be a watch dog at all times. He'll guarantee that until your meetings, Ruben won't bother you or your friends. I can be sure of that, unfortunately, if he's with me. It goes without saying that if you come to an agreement with Stanley, you'll never see or hear from Ruben again. You can imagine how I feel about Ruben guard dogging me, but it's non-negotiable…"

"It also means that you'll be off limits to us," Cash observes.

"Yes, one of the things he's concerned about is that I may have been disloyal to him with you, or I may help you or even align with you moving forward. This makes any further contact between us impossible."

"He's smart," the General observed.

"Yes, and I have to be very careful going forward, because he will kill me if he even suspects I'm untrustworthy."

"Okay then, we'll break off our contact with you, at least in the near term. Please give us a way to reach you if it's urgent."

"Yes, I will. I'll think of something and email it to you when I send you the banking information later today."

"We won't use it unless it's unavoidable."

"Thank you… As to your second question, he wouldn't even try to do this if he didn't think he could make a deal with you—so he's planning on offering something substantial. I already have bank account information on investors that he thinks may be moving Venezuelan military funds, and I'll pass that on to you right away. I know that he's willing to give you what he knows to keep you from putting his own business under a microscope. He'll explain to you that he hasn't personally been involved in Venezuelan military money, but he'll give you any of his investors who may have been. I don't think he's afraid of the Venezuelan military accusing him of theft. Off the record, my guess is that he's worrying about the IRS coming after him. He's afraid that you'll expose consequential tax issues, which I can't prove, but is certainly possible, and—this is, of course, confidential—that would explain the secrecy in all of his offshore corporations, and it would explain why he never reveals the identify of his investors, the identities of any other owners in his real estate ventures. I think that finally, he's worried that they'll charge him with tax evasion, even tax fraud, then perhaps close down and take possession of his real estate business."

"We're interested in finding the missing Venezuelan military money," General Lopez confirmed. "If he can put us in this direction, we'll leave him alone to handle his tax issues."

"Can I tell him that?"

"Yes," the General said.

"Good. I'll get back to you today with the other things we discussed and with a proposed meeting time. Can you meet in San Francisco or do you prefer to meet here?"

Cash answered, "Tell him we'd prefer to meet here. He can designate a time and a meeting place."

"Very well. This is the last time I will be able to talk with you on the phone unobserved. Ruben arrives today."

"We understand," Cash said.

"I appreciate your willingness to be helpful in this regard. Thank you, gentlemen." Alberto signed off.

****

"This is making me uneasy," General Lopez said after Alberto was gone.

"I agree," Callie added. "I don't understand what Stanley's after, and I don't trust Alberto."

"I agree, and I think Mario was right," Cash nodded. "I think he's up to something and he's buying time."

The General spoke up, "It is possible that he's simply the vehicle, the executer who's investing the stolen money, but why does he need time? He can send us on a wild goose chase—that is your word, yes? But what does he gain?"

"Do we believe that he's hiding tax fraud, that he's afraid of the IRS?" Callie asked.

"That's possible," Cash responded, "but I think it's unlikely. He's too careful. However, I definitely share your concerns about Alberto. We have no idea if what Alberto told us is even true, or if Stanley's actually intending to meet with us in five or six days… and we certainly don't know if, and why, he wants more time."

"We need to get quick answers to some of our questions."

"I have an idea. This is bold, but suppose we kidnap Ruben—we could do that tonight while he's babysitting Alberto—then tell Stanley that we'll only give him back if we can make a deal, and if we can get answers to our questions. If we can't, we'll send Ruben to face a miliary court martial investigation in Venezuela. Can we do that Mario?"

"Yes, Colonel Bolivar would do that. He could easily investigate him for collaborating on stealing the military money."

"That will make Stanley crazy. Then to add insult to injury, specifically, to keep him from buying time now, we tell Stanley we need to know his proposal right away, that we'd like to meet tomorrow morning on a Zoom call. That we'll return his man Ruben if, and only if, we can actually make a deal quickly. Tell him we need to know his investors. Can he prove that they are using Venezuelan military money? Tell him we want financial statements for all of his real estate developments and much more."

"He'll never agree." Callie shook her head.

"There's a tension for him. He won't want to give us that information, but he'll do almost anything to keep Ruben from going on trial in Venezuela."

"Is there anything he could do to threaten our people quickly to trade them for Ruben?" Callie asked.

"We'll have to warn everyone to be on full alert. The Macher can take that over."

General Lopez stood. "Don't ever underestimate this man. Remember he's fooled the entire Venezuelan military for the past five years."

"Point taken. Still, we need to play offense before he gets even further ahead of us. I say let's take Ruben tonight. I'll do it with Andre."

"I'll help you," the General added.

"I'm not sure that Generals in exile want to get involved in something like this."

"This one does… Let's make our plan."

"General, do you see why I adore this guy?" Callie asked, smiling wide.

"Yes, I do. I commented on you earlier. I told him that you reminded me of my own wife."

"Then I'm sure I'm in good company."

General Mario Lopez kissed Callie's hand.

****

Cash reached Andre at the airport in Miami. "I have another idea. I'm going to need your help tonight."

"Truthfully, you need my help every night."

"And you need a lobotomy… Now, just try and pay attention…"

"Wait, I have more info. I hung around the post office, and *Superman*'s Jimmy Olsen came in to pick up something, a final payment came to him through the PO box, though I didn't know that at the time. They send him cash in an envelope, so there's no checking account. It was dumb luck that I overheard him talking to the guy at the counter. Long story short, I braced him outside. Jimmy is just a kid, maybe twenty-five. I leaned on him, scared him a little. He didn't know anything. I did convince him to tell me what he did know."

"I bet you did."

"Relax, he was scared, not hurt. He did tell me that his job was to drop the mail in a locker at the train station in Santa Rosa. They give him a different locker for each visit. He has no idea when they pick it up, probably at random, unpredictable times. Last week, they called him, and said they wouldn't need his help any longer. This mail drop is over. That's all he knew."

"He's worried. He must know we're getting closer, and he's shutting down all possible access."

"You really think so, brainiac?"

"Asshole, just pay attention… Things have heated up and we're going on the offense. You, the General, and I are going to kidnap Ruben tonight. He's one of Stanley's DCGIM special forces thugs. He's likely one of the guys who killed Luis, killed Garcia, Luis' informant, killed Detective Rafael, kidnapped Alvaro and beat up Sara. He's going to be living at Alberto's house, keeping an eye on him. It's here in Miami, and I have the address. He's obviously very dangerous so we'll need to spend some time working it out. Can you come straight to our safe house and meet with the General and me this afternoon?"

"On my way, I should be there in half an hour… You know, even when you're serious, when you have new fresh ideas, even when you take charge and give clear, stern orders, you're still just such a pussy." Andre hung up.

Cash said something profane as Andre hung up, then called the Macher next. First, he filled him in.

When Cash finished, the Macher replied, "I'm guessing that after all of this, particularly freezing his bank account, my investment in his real estate development is on hold."

"That's my bet, and as soon as we take Ruben and threaten to send him to Venezuela to face a military court martial, it'll be old news. In the meantime, I'd like you to check in on all of our people who aren't here, our crew in Cuba. All hell is going to break lose, so bring in all of your Cuban people to make sure that our people are safe. You know who to contact, and I'll leave that up to you. It goes without saying that

Stanley is very smart and ruthless, so we need to be on full alert. Callie, incidentally, is here with me, so you don't have to be concerned about her. Please come by here or call in later after you've set it up. We need to figure out where to secure and hide Ruben, then figure out exactly what and how to tell Stanley, and, of course, your ideas are welcome."

****

Stanley had taken a call from Alberto.

Alberto was explaining, "I've had three offers, two are serious. Here's the one that meets most of your goals. It's from the Russell Group. They're reliable, discrete, accomplished and they can move quickly.

"Yes, I know of them. They would be a good choice."

"I agree. They'll pay seventy-five million now and another three hundred and fifty million over ten years—that's thirty-five million per year—for a total of four hundred and twenty-five million. You've committed three hundred million so far, including land under development. Interest on two hundred and twenty-five million (the difference between three hundred million and seventy-five million) at five percent for one year is eleven million two hundred and fifty thousand dollars. Interest on year two is two hundred twenty-five million, minus thirty-five million dllars, equals one hundred and ninety million, plus eleven million two hundred and fifty thousand, equals two hundred and one million and two hundred fifty thousand, times five percent, equals ten million and sixty-two thousand five hundred...and so on.

Over the entire ten years the loss of interest at five percent will be fifty-three million two hundred and eight thousand six hundred sixty-five. Four hundred twenty-five thousand, minus fifty-three million two hundred and eight thousand six hundred sixty-five, equals three hundred seventy-one million seven hundred and ninety-one thousand three hundred thirty-five. That means that after deducting the loss of interest, your three hundred million will eventually become three hundred seventy-one million seven hundred ninety-one thousand three hundred thirty-five. That's not a huge profit, about two and a half percent each year, but still approximately seventy-two million dollars more than you've spent. Will that be acceptable?"

"Under the circumstances, that will suffice. Do you think we should counter or try to close this deal as soon as possible."

"I told them we wanted their very best offer, that time was of the essence. They're excited to get these fine properties at a discount, and they understand that they have to move discretely and quickly. My opinion is that if you're satisfied with these numbers, we should close it right away. I don't think we can do any better or more quickly with an equally competent buyer, and this offer could unwind. If you accept this offer and tell them you're putting their competition on hold, I believe we can have a binding agreement signed in three days. We'll need to allow them more time to do all their inspections, detail confirmations, etc., but that's a formality."

"Let's do it right away then… Today is Tuesday, I want at least thirty-seven five into a bank I'll designate, non-refundable, by Friday." Stanley/Brendan hung up.

***

Cash, Callie, General Lopez and Andre were sitting around the island in the kitchen. "Should we tell Alberto about our plans for tonight?" Cash wondered. "It will happen, after all, at his house." "I wouldn't." The General replied. "I think it's safer if he doesn't know, and truthfully, my instincts say he's not our guy."

Cash nodded. "I think your instincts are right. Even if he is, if he doesn't know, and we put him down, make him unconscious, tie him up, blindfold him and leave him, immobile, on the couch, that will keep him out of it. At least, he won't be blamed by Stanley."

"Let's take both of them, quickly, then leave Alberto behind," Andre suggested.

"End of the day, Stanley will know that we have Ruben, and it won't hurt us for Alberto to confirm that we were there, that we took them by surprise," Cash added.

Andre suggested. "He doesn't know me. Let's set up some ruse whereby I'm bringing something, likely from the General, and he'll answer the door. I'll take him right there, put him out quickly. The rest of you can break in through the back, earlier, and close to the same time, take Ruben from behind."

General Lopez nodded. "Yes, I can make that call, and I have an idea about what I can send to him. It'll be something about our Cayman Island investigation, that he'll want to see."

Callie spoke up, "When you get Ruben, tie him down, then force open his mouth, wide, and set it so he can't close it. When you're finished, I'm going to pour my secret cocktail down his throat. I'll make him swallow dog urine, dog feces, raw chicken fat, olive oil, tabasco, and so on. Basically, I'm going to kick his ass for what he did to Sara."

****

Stanley had assembled his crew in his spacious living room. Tim, Erik, and Carlos were there. "I've been putting together the next phase. Once we make our deal for the real estate, we'll fade away for a time while I finalize next steps. They've gotten way too close—blowing up my boat, bringing in the Venezuelan General, unexpectedly and especially troubling, freezing my bank account. Now, they're trying to find me. Someone found the mail runner from San Francisco to Santa Rosa and questioned him. He didn't know anything, but that puts them fifty miles away. It's time to disappear. As you know, we have another boat, a Sunseeker 120 Yacht, securely stored in a boat house in San Francisco. It's a beautiful boat that comfortably accommodates ten guests with cabin configurations, each with an ensuite bath. Johan will be back this evening. Under his direction, let's be prepared to move onto the yacht in two or three days. I'll want Tim, Erik, and Johan with me on the boat.

Alberto will finish up the real estate deal and the transfer of the initial payment before we leave. I brought in my personal lawyer, Carl Stone, in New York City, to oversee Alberto on the real estate deal. You all know him and understand that he's very capable and absolutely reliable. Alberto also knows him, and he'll cooperate, helping Carl get whatever he needs to confirm and sign off on Alberto's work. If that takes more than three days, that is to say Friday, I'll delay my meeting with our adversaries. In any event, I have no intention of ever meeting with them.

Once we're at sea, I'll send Carlos to join Ruben in Miami. I'll want them to eliminate our enemies, quickly. If my information is up to date, that starts with Cash Logan, Callie James, and their colleague Andre. I'm thinking that may end all of their harassing inquiries. While we're at sea, Ruben and Carlos will keep an eye on the situation. If others, like General Lopez or Cash's daughter, Sara, or her husband, Alvaro, persist, we'll deal with them as well. As a precaution, I want Erik and Tim to confirm their people in Cuba, the people who are helping them there and identify other friends here, such as their babysitter, the diamond trader, or anyone else that we can use to put pressure on them should the need arrive. Any questions?"

Erik spoke up, "Do you know where we're going or how long we'll be gone?"

"Yes, to the first. No, to the second. But I'm not ready to discuss either of those things yet. It's best if no one knows our plans until we're out to sea. Those who are staying in Miami don't ever need to know our location. Those of you who are going, be ready to leave as scheduled, and if you stay with me, be ready to be away as long as a year."

"Do you think General Lopez and the others will back off?"

"Unlikely, but they'll pause for a beat to assess the situation. The girl and her husband will have to come back from Cuba. The General will wait for them. Once they've reassembled, if they persist, we'll deal with it."

"Will they send others to look for us?"

"Yes, certainly, but the people who know anything at all will be gone. None of the new people will know what we've done, and, most importantly, they won't know where we are. We are going to disappear, vanish where we'll never be found."

CHAPTER FIVE

General Lopez had called Alberto, politely explaining that he had a letter from a military investigator, the Colonel that he worked with, who was requesting specifics detailing various wire transactions in and out of the Cayman Island account that they'd frozen. Out of courtesy, he wanted to pass it on, and discuss it, before deciding exactly what to send on. He'd have one of his men, Andre, bring it by this evening. Was 7:30 p.m. too late?" he asked, politely.

"Not at all," Alberto had agreed, appreciatively.

By 7:10 p.m., Andre, the recognized expert in these matters, had furtively spent thirty minutes scouting out the back of the house. Earlier this afternoon, he'd pretended to be a building inspector and secured a blueprint of the house, then chosen the safest entry way to break in. Now, at 7:15 p.m., he was explaining the recommended point of entry for General Lopez and Cash. Once inside, they'd be in a dark laundry room. Andre had showed them earlier on the plan where they could wait safely in the dark laundry room until they heard the front door. Next, he passed his preferred tools for opening a glass sliding side door to Cash who led General Mario Lopez behind a bush that provided cover to enter in the remote back. Andre had already made a small hole above the sliding door and disconnected the alarm sensor. He'd long ago learned how to bypass the detector without setting off the alarm. He'd tried explaining that to Cash several times but eventually gave up and resigned himself to doing it himself when he was working with Cash. This arrangement apparently worked for both of them.

Cash and the General were safely secure inside when they heard the front door. They crept along the hallway that opened into the entryway where they saw Alberto opening the front door, welcoming in Andre.

Andre held an envelope that he handed to Alberto. Ruben was standing, watching carefully, perhaps ten yards behind Alberto. Everything that happened next happened quickly, almost simultaneously. When Andre saw Cash and the General stepping softly behind Ruben, he swiftly kicked Alberto's groin with his metal prosthetic leg, driving him to his knees, barely able to breathe. As Ruben pulled his gun, Cash sapped the back of his head with a heavy iron truncheon. As Ruben fell, he turned toward Cash. Before Ruben could fire, General Lopez was already on him, injecting a loaded syringe into the side of his neck. He injected a shot of Etorphine, a synthetic opioid, used to tranquilize large animals. Unconsciousness was almost instantaneous. Then, Andre wrapped a rag, dosed in chloroform, behind Alberto's mouth and nose. While Cash and General Lopez shackled Ruben's feet and wrists, Andre held the chloroform behind Alberto for three or four minutes until he, too, was unconscious.

Cash brought their car in front of the house, and he and the General managed to place the shackled, unconscious, Ruben into their trunk. Before locking it, they secured a gag around his mouth. Inside, Cash and Andre tied Alberto's hands and feet with rope, then lay him, also unconscious, on the living room coach.

Back at the safe house, Cash called the Macher. "We've got their killer, Ruben. He's shackled. We locked him in our safe house until we can raise Alberto and communicate with Stanley later."

"Sounds good. I talked with Alvaro and Sara, then Nestor, and he brought in two other expert security people. We moved Alvaro, Sara, and their son, your grandson, Y.C., to another safe house Nestor had access to. They're well protected, and no one knows where they are. I don't need to tell you that you have to be very careful with Ruben. He's very capable and extremely dangerous."

"We shackled him lying on the bed in the spare room. He's also chained to the floor and to the wall behind him. He's blindfolded so he won't know where he is and gagged so he can't talk. When he wakes up, we intend to take off the gag and force his mouth open so he can't close it.

Andre has dental tools, bite blocks, to do that. Callie has prepared an unbelievably disgusting drink to force down his throat. It's payback for our friends, especially Sara."

"I'm on my way. Tell her I'll look forward to seeing that… Dare I ask what's in it?"

"I'm sure she'd be happy to wait for you, and if you really want to know, she'll give you the details."

"How about a little hint?"

"Jesus, Itzac, you're an old, wise, learned, scholar… What the hell are you doing?"

"This man and his cohort killed Alvaro's cousin, Luis, and Garcia, who took the photo. They badly beat your daughter, and kidnapped Alvaro. They just killed Detective Rafael… and that's just what this man has done lately… What you have here is a truly evil, despicable, unfeeling human being. You're never too old—and I can see you have yet to learn this—you're never too old to savor seeing such a hateful man taste Callie's considered, just revenge. Son, that's an old man passing on learned wisdom… Truthfully boychik, it's lyrical, it's biblical."

"I'll never tell anyone that you said that Itzac… However, for old time's sake, here's a taste—dog urine, dog feces, how she got it I didn't ask, raw chicken fat, olive oil, tabasco and more…"

"That's your girl… Tell her I can't wait. It's times like this that create unforgettable memories."

"Particularly for deviant torture aficionados…"

****

At about 9:30 p.m. ET, Cash called Miguel in Dallas. "Miguel, it's Cash Logan. I don't have time to catch up, but I need a favor right away… Thank you… I need you to contact Alberto's secretary. She needs to come to his house right now. She'll need a key… Good… He's tied up, barely conscious, on the couch, but he's fine, unharmed. We need her to untie him then have her call me with him… Sooner the better…

You don't want to know... Thank you... Hope you're well, I'll call you to fill you in when this is over." Cash signed off.

Cash nodded "yes" to the General in the living room, then opened the spare room, poked in to see Ruben wide awake, crying, coughing, fighting for breaths and making guttural noises. Andre had pried open his mouth with dental bite blocks, his head was tied back to the bedframe so he couldn't move it. The Macher and Andre were watching Callie stirring her cocktail again, vigorously, then pouring the rest of the portion slowly, steadily, down Ruben's throat. He made a retching noise as he tried, unsuccessfully, to throw the disgusting concoction out of his throat. His tears were flowing, and his stomach was heaving. Callie continued carefully pouring her mixture slowly into his open mouth as she said, "This is for Sara, the woman you beat up, for Luis, Garcia and Rafael, who you killed, and for Alvaro who you kidnapped. Remember this before you ever touch one of our friends again...You heartless bastard! And if you ever come back at any of us, anytime, I'll feed you this potion again, until you smother, until I strangle you to death with it." She finished pouring, as he turned bright red, gasping for breath.

****

A half hour later, Alberto called, barely recovered from being unconscious. "It was you, wasn't it," were the first words out of his mouth.

"Yes, and we have a message we want you to give to your boss, right away," Cash replied.

"After what you did, why should I get in the middle of this?"

"Don't even start this. We set this up so that you're in the clear. We don't believe that you're genuinely on our side, but we still protected you. Short answer – you have to do this, precisely what we ask, or we'll make you a co-conspirator... Are you understanding me?"

"Yes, go ahead."

"Please tell Stanley—we still call him that—that we have Ruben, that we're going to turn him over to the Venezuelan military, for a court martial, if he doesn't meet with us tomorrow, on a Zoom call.

At this meeting we need to know his proposal right away. We'll return his man Ruben if, and only if, we can actually make a deal quickly. Tell him to make that deal we need to know his investors. We need him to convince us that they are using Venezuelan military money. Tell him we also want financial statements for all of his real estate developments, tax returns and so on."

"He'll never agree to that."

"Then get him thinking about Ruben telling all he knows at a military court martial. Tell him that Ruben will spend the rest of his life, or worse, if he doesn't tell them everything, especially the details of what happened with the stolen three hundred and fifty million dollars of Venezuelan military money. If you won't do that convincingly, we'll send you to Venezuela with Ruben to face that same court martial. You've betrayed my trust, Alberto, and I will send you to this court martial if you disappoint me. Do you understand what I'm saying?"

"Yes… I'll try to reach him right now."

"Call me after you talk with him."

****

"That's right sir, they have Ruben," Alberto explained to Stanley.

There was a long silence before Stanley spoke. When he finally did speak his voice was very slow, understated, and precise, a sure sign that he was livid. "And what are they threatening to do, and what are they asking me to do, exactly?"

"They're threatening to send Ruben to Venezuela to face a military court martial. They want to meet with you tomorrow, on Zoom. They'll only return Ruben if, and only if, they can actually make a deal with you quickly at that meeting. To do that, they'll need to know all of your investors. They want you to demonstrate, convincingly, that some of your investors are using Venezuelan military money. Then they want financial statements for all of your real estate developments, tax returns and more."

"You're certain you have this exactly right?"

"Yes, I paid careful attention."

"I see… Tell them, then, that I'll contact them, through you, tomorrow morning… I want you to be available at all times."

"Yes, sir, I will."

Stanley hesitated, pensive, then asked, "How close are we to concluding our real estate deal?"

"I'd guess two days."

"I want half of the seventy-five million, that's thirty-seven million five hundred, deposited in my Panama account—the one I gave to you earlier—tomorrow morning. I want the other half one day after signing our agreement. I want the agreement signed tomorrow, day after tomorrow, latest. Can you accomplish that?"

"Yes, I think we can sign day after tomorrow."

"Get this right, Alberto. Right now, you're hanging by a thread." He hung up.

Stanley looked out the window, onto his lit patio. He knew what he had to do. He called Erik. "Get everyone up here into the living room, and I'll want everything you've learned about people we can touch to put pressure on them. The need to do that has arrived."

****

Erik, Tim, Johan and Carlos were all seated around the coffee table in the living room. Erik was making his report on what he'd learned so far. He had the name and location of the babysitter. He reported Itzac, "The Macher's," address in NYC, he was still looking for some of Alvaro's friends in Miami, when he got to Callie, Stanley stopped him. "Does she have any close friends or relatives?" He asked.

"She has a teenaged son, in college, eighteen or nineteen."

"What did you learn about him?"

"I was sure that he would interest you, so I focused on him. I called Callie's restaurant and explained to the maître d' that I was a friend of his from high school and that I needed to find him. I'll spare you the details, but he gave me a name and a phone number of a friend of his in Seattle.

I learned from his friend that he was off in college, at Berkeley, and he gave me his dorm. I found his address."

"Good. I want you and Carlos to take him tonight, right away. Don't hurt him, simply bring him tied, blindfolded, to our San Francisco bungalow. Call me when he's secured in the basement there. Carlos, I want you to go on to Miami tonight, right away, to be ready as I negotiate Ruben's release."

****

At 6:00 a.m. PT / 9:00 a.m. ET, Alberto called Cash. Cash was alone in the kitchen having coffee, when Alberto said, "I heard from Stanley. Sit down… He has taken Callie's son, Lew."

"Shit! God fucking damnit! You tell him right away that if he touches Lew, hurts him in any way, I'll kill him. I swear I will."

"I'll tell him—"

Cash interrupted, "Where is Lew, now?"

"He's in San Francisco. He's a captive, locked up, under guard."

"Is he hurt?"

"In Stanley's words, 'no, he's not hurt yet.'"

"What does this man want?"

"He's furious. He won't talk with you; he won't even communicate further until you exchange Ruben for Callie's son. And he explicitly said to tell you that if you ever threaten to bring his people to a Venezuelan court martial again, he'll kill you."

"We'll come back to that… Now, this changes everything. I want Lew back, right away. We'll trade Ruben for him today. I'll go to San Francisco and get Lew. We won't release Ruben until I know Lew's safe. We'll free Ruben at a distance, in the back of the second floor of the parking garage three blocks north of Alvaro's blown-up burned-down bar, The Midnight Mirage. Set this up right away. I'll be in San Francisco this afternoon. Do it right now. Call me back right away with the specifics." Cash hung up, called Callie, who came out from the bedroom.

She took one look at Cash and asked, already upset, "What's wrong babe?"

He took her in his arms, sat her down at the counter, "They have Lew."

Callie screamed, "No… Oh no…" She was crying now, holding onto him, tightly. "Is he okay?"

"I think so. We'll trade him for Ruben this afternoon. I already set it up with Alberto. I'll go to San Francisco to make the trade. I'll make sure he's okay. I need to get a flight right away."

Callie screamed, again. "Agh!!!... Dear God… how did they find my son? How could we miss that?"

"I was asking myself the same thing. They're very smart, very experienced, expert at getting info. But it's my fault. I foolishly didn't think he was in danger. I never thought they would know about him, or be able to find him. I should have put someone on to protect him. I'm feeling awful. When this is over, we'll get out of this. It's gone too far. Sara was right before, and it feels like I can't stay clear from putting my family in danger. There's no excuse. I'm so sorry."

"It's all of our fault. Let's just get him back safely, then we can rethink this, the whole thing… In the meantime, bear with me. I'm terrified, beside myself with worry that they might hurt him. What if they learn what I did to Ruben?" Callie started crying again, tears flowing.

Cash held her. "Babe, I'll take care of this… I'll tell Andre to clean Ruben up, tape his mouth so shut that he can't talk right away. We'll get Lew back before they learn what happened."

"You better get that right, babe…"

"I get that. Don't worry."

"Don't worry? Let's get to the airport, I'm going with you."

"Right, what am I thinking? I'll get two tickets. I'm calling now."

He turned as Andre came into the front door, carrying donuts. "They've got Lew," he told Andre. "We're going to trade him for Ruben. We're on our way to San Francisco to make the exchange. They'll give us Lew when they see Ruben, at a distance. I set that up in back of the second floor of the parking garage three blocks north of Alvaro's burned-out bar… I need you to clean up Ruben, then tape his mouth so thoroughly that he won't be able to talk when they get him. Use sophisticated, very strong glue if you have to. We have to be sure that he won't be able to tell what Callie did to him before we get Lew back. When you're confident that you've managed that, that they'll be able to make the trade before they'll learn what happened, then you can bring him to the designated place for the exchange. I'll get you the precise time soon."

"Is Lew okay?"

"So they say. I'll let you know after we get him."

"Good. I'll take care of delivering Ruben intact. I know how to do what you need. No problem. What else can I do?"

"Just fill in the Macher. Tell him I'll call him soon. I'll call you as soon as I know the specifics."

"Godspeed," Andre nodded to Cash, blew a kiss to Callie.

****

Cash had finished buying the tickets and he and Callie were in his car, going to the airport when the phone rang again. Alberto was back saying, "He'll make the exchange today at 4:00 p.m. PT in San Francisco. Lew will be released in front of the train station. Stanley's man will be in Miami to pick up Ruben in the second floor of the garage three blocks north of Alvaro's former bar. You'll be able to see Lew from a distance. Once Ruben has been seen, also from a distance, both of them will be released simultaneously. Both you and the man picking up Ruben will be in contact with his man Erik by phone. Do you concur?"

"Yes. I'm adding one more essential thing. This is important. It's now clear to me that this is out of control, bad for both of us. I'm proposing a cease fire, a truce, after the exchange. I'm willing to back off, leave him alone. I'll even withdraw from the investigation of the missing money. To do that I'll need evidence that Stanley, Ruben, and his other men will leave us alone. Period. I'll want one of my men to watch Ruben and the man who picks him up, both of them, get on a plane to San Francisco.

Then I'll want credible guarantees from Stanley, guarantees that he'll be able to deliver demonstrably, that I'll be able to rely on. I'll leave it up to him to tell me how he can do that. I, in turn, will demonstrate how he can rely on my side of this bargain. I'm on my way to the airport now, but you can call me in the next hour, before I get on the plane, with his suggestion. You can tell him I'm serious about ending this right now. I mean this, and I, for one will back off. It has to stop before any more people die, before I have to kill him, before he has to kill me… Alberto, you know how I feel about you. You know I was willing to send you to a Venezuelan court martial. That said, you can help yourself if you give me a true assessment. Can this truce work?"

"I can tell you what I think… I know that he's focusing on other things. I also can tell that you've infuriated him. That could only happen if he's worried about you. I'd guess that if you give him meaningful, testable assurances that you will walk away, let him go his own way, he'll respond in kind. You're both too smart to be at war. Neither of you need this."

"Tell him that I'll work out the truce with you. Later today, after the exchange. Please call me after you talk with him."

****

From the car, Cash called the Macher who said straight off, "I heard the bad news from Andre… I'm glad you're going to get Lew."

"We'll get him, but I'm afraid that's just the beginning."

"We're thinking the same thing. We have to face facts here—they're just too fast. Unless we change directions, it's just a matter of time before more of us start dying."

"Yes, I need to negotiate some kind of truce. I think to do that, I have to back off. I have to genuinely step away from this."

"For now, I agree—the cost is just too high."

"I'll tell the General, and I'm sure he'll understand. He may pause, but he won't back off."

"No, let me talk with him. I'll ask him to take a break, at least until Lew is safe and you've made your cease fire. When Lew is safe, and you've made your truce, we can revisit all of this."

"Thank you, that helps me."

***

At the airport, while they were waiting for their flight, Cash took Alberto's call.

"Stanley, too, will consider a truce. He'll keep his people away from you, guaranteed, provided that you demonstrate to him that you'll end your investigation into his affairs. Specifically, he knows it's too late to undo the freeze on his account, but he wants you to withdraw from the investigation. To demonstrate that, to make evident your sincere intentions, he wants you to leave Florida, indefinitely."

"If that makes a truce possible, and if he'll make a comparable gesture, I will do that. I will move back to Seattle with Callie and stay away from Florida. I'll also direct my people to stay away from Florida and stop investigating Stanley's affairs. You also have my word that I'll withdraw from the investigation. I have an idea about how we both can confirm our respective promises, and I'll spell it out once I learn what Stanley will do to protect me, my family and my friends."

"I think he'll be satisfied with your return to Seattle and some way to verify that you don't return to Florida. It goes without saying that if he finds that you're investigating his affairs by phone, or any other way, this truce is over."

"I will not put this truce in jeopardy, but I need to know how I can rely on his promise to stop his people from harassing me and my family."

"He's willing to guarantee that. He said that if you'd genuinely back off, he and his people would, too. If you move away, if you don't express even curiosity about his affairs, business and otherwise, he'll promise, he'll ensure, to leave you and your family alone. He'll make Seattle, and Cuba, if your family stays there, off limits to all of his people wherever they are. This is an all or nothing deal, for both of you. He'll do whatever you require to enforce his part. You can set it up to monitor that, so that a single infringement by him dissolves your commitment, which is obviously important to him, and has other adverse consequences, such as reopening your investigation. He's open to your suggestions as to how he might convince you of that."

"This is encouraging. It's sounding possible. Who can monitor both sides of this arrangement?"

"I will supervise the truce with you and his righthand man, Erik, if we can specify what it involves."

"I'll also want my man, Detective Ed Samter, to monitor as well."

"I'll check in with him regularly."

"OK… After the exchange we should spell that out… Where is Stanley?"

"I don't know that, and he certainly won't tell you that, but I can confirm with him that it's far away from Florida or Seattle. I can tell you that he wants to focus on other things. He'd like for this truce to work."

"To that end, here's my one further idea to police this cease fire, for both of us. It works with what we've discussed. I'd like his man Erik to check in regularly with me. He can confirm, giving me specifics, including location, that his people are living with our agreement—I'll want verifiable reports. During these calls, I can confirm that I'm in Seattle and that me and my people are out of the investigation, also providing specifics. This truce works best if we are in regular contact and discuss compliance and unexpected events. Regular contact will also establish the trust that will help make this work. Each of us will check in separately with you after each of our calls. I'll also ask you to call Ed Samter after that, as I mentioned.

"No problem."

"Please talk again with Stanley, then let's you and I talk again after the exchange and confirm our agreement and work out any further details."

"I'll speak again with Stanley and talk with you after the exchange."

****

At 3:30 p.m. PT, Cash and Callie were in a rented car parked across the train station in San Francisco. At 3:58 p.m., he got a call from Erik.

"Our man is in the parking garage you specified. He'd like your man to show Ruben."

"I'll call my man and give him the go ahead, as soon as your man here shows Lew."

"In precisely two minutes, at four p.m., we can show both men. The moment Lew walks outside the train station, Ruben will be shown. My man is on hold waiting for me to send a signal."

At precisely 4:00 p.m., Cash saw Lew, handcuffed and gagged stepping in front of the train station. He signaled Andre to show Ruben. Andre took him out of the car. He, too, was handcuffed, and his mouth was muzzled, covered by a covid mask. Both Cash and Carlos approved their designated captive at the same time, and both men were released, though still handcuffed, gagged or muzzled. The agreement called for the keys to the handcuffs to be placed in each man's pocket, and after Lew crossed the street, Cash quickly unlocked the hand cuffs then hugged him warmly. Cash then hurried him into the car where Callie was waiting eagerly in the back seat to welcome Lew into her arms. Cash drove away hurriedly, wanting to be far away before they figured out how to open Ruben's mouth.

Lew's first sentence to Cash was, "It's not easy being your stepson."

"I'm very sorry about the trouble I keep causing for you. Before I explain more about it, and about what I intend to do about it, will you please assure us that you weren't mistreated."

Callie added, "Yes, please, reassure us that you're really OK."

"If you call being locked up, gagged and handcuffed in some kind of cellar but not being harmed "OK," then I'm OK. The good news is that this isn't the first time that one of your enemies has kidnapped me. It was better than being locked in the trunk, like the last time, and I'm at least getting used to being rescued. The answer to your question, mom, is that I really am OK. Nevertheless, I hope I don't have your skills at choosing a partner."

"I understand."

"I appreciate that... now, I need a minute to call Lisa."

Callie handed her son her phone as Cash's phone rang.

"Yes, Erik, you'll be able to open Ruben's mouth. He'll be fine... Don't start with me. He's a killer, and he's killed three of our friends, badly beaten my daughter and kidnapped her husband. You can tell Stanley that a little unpleasant, but not lethal, payback was nothing like what he deserved. Remind him that we are not killing people... Ruben is a monster. Still, he's going to be just fine, and truthfully, he's lucky to be alive...so damnit, just lay off, let this go, or this truce will never work... yes, I do appreciate your help... I tell you what—I'll send a message to Stanley that your understanding made this truce possible."

****

Cash, Callie and Lew were at the airport. They were going back to Seattle. They needed to get back home, confirm the truce, take a deep breath and rethink many things. Mostly, Cash and Callie felt very fortunate that Lew was fine, and without saying it, they both new that they'd been lucky—and somehow, they also knew that they'd pushed their luck far enough.

Cash called the Macher again from the airport. He'd called him earlier to tell him Lew was fine, but they had more to discuss. "Before we talk, I'm putting Lew on the line, he wants to say hello."

He gave Lew the phone. "Itzac, I wanted to hear your voice, though I have to say, I'd like to talk with you more when I'm not getting out of some life-threatening situation."

"Lew, it's great to talk with you regardless of the situation. I'm relieved and delighted that you're fine."

"Thank you, Itzac. I need a little help. My stepdad listens to you. As you know, I love him very much, but this time, it was just too often. I don't want to live in fear that some monster is going to kidnap me, maybe kill me, because of what Cash is doing. I will, of course, talk with both him and my mom about this, but will you lend a hand? This needs to end."

"Yes. We all agree with you. I'll be seeing your mom and your stepdad when they get back, and this is the first item on the agenda. If they agree, I'm sure you'd be welcome to be a part of those conversations, and I'll be as helpful as I can."

"Good, I'd like that. I'll ask them."

"Good to talk with you, Lew. Please put Cash back on, I have more to discuss with him. I'll see you when you're back…"

Cash started right in, "How was your conversation with General Lopez?"

"It went well. He understands what you're doing, and he'll back off until you work out your truce. I think he'll even give you some extra time, but he won't walk away from his efforts to recover the money."

"I understand. I promised Stanley that I, and my—the word I used was 'people'—my people would back off. What I said exactly was, 'I'll also direct my people to stay away from Florida and stop investigating Stanley's affairs.' I'm sure that includes Callie, you, Andre, Alvaro, Sara, and Miguel. I don't think it covers the General. Let me talk with him, let me make sure that I'm clear with Stanley, and then perhaps we can make his work less noticeable, at least for a while. Depending on what that entails, let's even think about whether there's a discrete way for you to help him. Let's talk about that when I'm back. I'll call him tomorrow."

****

At 9:00 a.m. PT / noon ET, Alberto got a call from Stanley. It was actually a response from the code that Alberto had sent earlier. "I received the initial payment," Stanley said right off.

"You should receive the second payment, bringing the total to seventy-five million, later today. I just received the signed memorandum agreement," Alberto reported. "Give me the number you'd like me to use, and I'll scan it and email it to you right away. Read it, then sign it, and send it back to me. The money will come soon after. Importantly, the signed agreement is legally final, binding and irrevocable. We will nevertheless finish the final agreement soon after, and get it signed, but it's a formality. I did that so you wouldn't have to worry about the details."

"Excellent. As you know, on a deal like this, we won't be finished until Carl Stone signs off. I'm assuming that you've been copying him on everything and generally keeping him up to date."

"Yes, of course. As always, he's been very smart and easy to deal with."

"Good. I've asked him to review everything, even the little things, that you've done. The memorandum, the correspondence, the notes you have on your calls with Cash Logan, anything else you and I decided to do before closing, and of course the final agreement. Is he up to date?"

"Yes, absolutely, as of last night."

"Please send him anything else that might be outstanding, or that you might have missed, today, FedEx."

"I'll do that as soon as we're off the phone."

"Good. What are the next steps?"

"My associates—I have actually put four people on it—and I are finishing the more detailed agreement. Now that the property has been sold, there are some other documents that I'll have to file with the county clerk. I can delay that for several days, but once I file them, the sale will be public record. The buyers will have things to file too, so if you want this to proceed as planned, you should be ready for some attention, some inquiries."

"I'll expect you to handle any questions, any publicity. I also want you to delay whatever you have to file and anything the buyer will be filing for three more days, that is to say two days after tomorrow. Can you arrange that?"

"Yes, I think so. It's not a problem for me, and I'm sure the buyer will wait if I ask. They're pleased about this deal, and they've been trying to accommodate our timing."

"That helps. I'd like to wrap up our cease fire with Cash Logan and his people before they learn about this deal. You've asserted that the real estate deal in the memorandum agreement is final, unchangeable. Can I rely on that?"

"It is, absolutely unalterable."

"For your sake, I hope so. So, you know, Carl Stone will also confirm that after he reviews it tonight. I'd also like you to send him anything you have to file, even if it's several days off. If he wants changes, I'll expect you to make them right away."

"Of course."

"Regarding the specifics of the cease fire, we're already close to having a truce—the exchange of prisoners was successfully completed. I've reviewed Cash's suggestions and discussed them with Erik. We think this truce, as monitored, can work. We'll accept you and Cash's designated person, Detective Samter, as follow up supervisors/monitors after Erik and Cash talk regularly. Erik will follow up the details with you today. I'll want the deal for the truce in a letter—specifically, the termination of the investigation and the monitoring provisions. I don't want any confusion or second guessing. I'd like the letter to finally say—and though this is not meant to have legal meaning, it is, however, plainly important—it should say that we've agreed to unspecified consequences, to be determined by each of us independently in the event there's a violation of the agreement by the other party. They will notice that and take it seriously. Please send it to Carl and to me as soon as you're satisfied with it."

"That will go out right away."

"I hope that this can be worked out successfully this afternoon."

"This is an unusual letter. I think, however, that both parties will understand such a letter. It will be short and straightforward."

"Good. Erik will also be your regular contact for the real estate sale. I'll return the signed agreements to you right away, and I'll let you know when the next payment arrives. Call Cash and wrap this up, talk with Erik if Cash raises anything new. You and I will talk later… You're on track. It's in your interests, it's, in fact, essential to your well-being that you stay on course."

****

At 10:00 a.m. PT / 1:00 p.m. ET Cash called General Mario Lopez. "Mario, I imagine you've already heard from Itzac, and he told you about Callie's son's kidnapping and our exchange Ruben for Lew."

"I'm so sorry about Callie's son, and I'm very happy he's now safe. I do understand what you did, and why you did it. Please tell me more specifics."

"Part of the deal I'm trying to close includes a truce between Stanley and me. I simply can't continue to put my family members at risk."

"I understand. How can I help?" The General asked.

"I think it would help me make the truce if you'd back off, too. At least for another week or more, until the cease fire is in place, and working well. After that, we can revisit this, perhaps come up with other options."

"I understand, and of course I'll do that, for a week or ten days. What will the truce look like?"

"At the very least, it will mean that I'll have to back away from all of the things that you and I have been working on together—freezing his bank account in the Cayman Islands, bringing some of Stanley's people like Ruben and others to a court martial in Venezuela, investigating the real estate holdings and so on. I won't be able to work further, to follow through with you, with any of those things."

"As you can imagine, I won't walk away from my efforts to recover the money… but let's postpone our conversation about that until after the truce is working. In the meantime, I'd like to do more research on his real estate investments. Can you recommend someone who won't draw attention to it, if he or she helps me with that?"

"Let me talk with the Macher, then one of us will call you back. It may take a couple of days."

"That's fine."

"Thank you, your sensitivity and your help means a lot to Callie and me."

"It's the least I could do. I know what it means when one of your children is in danger. Nothing is worse. You're a valued friend and I'll wait to hear from you."

"Likewise… I'll be in touch."

****

The Macher arrived while Callie, Cash and Lew were eating lunch. They were seating around the island in the kitchen, eating Callie's homemade crab salad with fresh local crab, green onions, chopped red onions, peas, sliced hard-boiled egg, other special ingredients, and Callie's own secret creamy dressing. They invited the Macher to join them. He took one look at Callie's crab salad, smiled wide, sat down and helped himself.

While he was still serving himself a generous portion, Callie explained, "Cash and I have decided to go back to Seattle and stay here. It's part of our truce with Stanley. We're also going to invite Sara, Alvaro & Y.C. to join us when they can. Lew will be going back to college."

"As part of the truce," Cash added, "we'd like you and Andre to drop the investigation into Stanley's real estate. Will that work for you?"

"For now, I think it's a good idea. Have you talked with the General?"

"Yes. He'll back off for at least a week, but he won't give up trying to find the money. In the meantime, he wants to hire someone discrete to do some research on Stanley's Florida real estate investments. I told him I'd ask you to recommend someone."

"I do have someone. She's a writer, and to make extra money, part time, she does specific jobs for me in New York City. She's discrete, and she can poke around without drawing any attention. I'll ask her to say she's doing an article for some minor wealthy old people's retirement magazine about exclusive, Naples, Florida real estate retirement opportunities."

"That works. Make sure Stanley doesn't even notice it."

"That's easy enough. Her name is Nancy Lee, and I'll call her today."

"Let's talk in a few days about the General. We need to think through what he can and can't do and your involvement."

"That's going to be complicated."

"I agree." Callie nodded. "Still, can I change the subject?"

"Yes, let's finish this later," the Macher replied.

"Okay. You remember the conversation we all had when we took time off on the boat?"

"Yes, of course, you were working hard to stay out of danger."

"Yes, and we followed what we agreed, especially Cash, and it was working until Alvaro's cousin, Luis, showed up."

"Yes, I remember, and this recent trouble led to Sara being attacked."

"Right, and then people were killed and kidnapped."

Lew jumped in, "Is there any way to get off this terrible trajectory?"

"I've been thinking about that," Cash replied. "And truthfully, I think if you have the kind of relationships we have, if you're able to help friends and loved ones… I mean, even if you avoid conflict in your work, as we have, if you're simply active in the world, some of this can happen. Look at Sara and Alvaro… I think that walking away, as we're doing now, may be the most effective deterrent."

The Macher nodded. "I think he's right. Unless you stop living an active, interesting life, there's always some possibility of some unexpected danger."

"Still, I'd like to do what we can to protect the next generation, and their children, from the frequency of danger that we experience," Callie said. "That should be possible."

"I hope so," Lew said. "If I'm going to get kidnapped, I'd like it to be for something that I've done, that I've chosen to do."

Cash nodded. "That's reasonable, but, I think, impossible to guarantee. I, for one, will try to keep you out of it and, if necessary, protect you from it."

"Good, but so far that's not working," Lew opined, matter of fact.

Callie touched her son's shoulder. "I think it's working more than it used to, and maybe it can work even more going forward, if everyone is mindful of it."

"Convince me," Lew challenged all three of them.

"Being aware of the dangers and trying to keep the next generation out of it, is, at least, a beginning," the Macher offered.

"Yes," Cash agreed. "But truthfully, I think we have to admit that my history and the histories of my friends like Andre and the Macher make these issues arise more often."

"And that's what I keep getting caught up in."

Cash spoke up again, "Well, I can help with that by giving you a heads up whenever me and my loved ones and friends might be targeted. I'll also send someone like Andre to look after you. Finally, I'm going to do my best to simply walk away before any danger gets that far..."

"All good, but so far, it's just not good enough..."

"Truthfully, though it's the best I know how to do, you're right, it's not enough. Unfortunately, you can't simply eliminate the dangers if you live near a possibly live volcano, or a common earthquake area, or a place that's prone to mosquitos carrying malaria... in your case, dangerous people are still a real, though I hope less frequent, part of your life."

"I love all of you guys, and you're all very smart, but damnit, you're not really solving the problem."

Callie sighed. "Son, I think that since I've lived with Cash, especially after we all lived for almost a year on the boat, I learned that there really isn't a final, ultimate solution for this problem. We are doing better, we'll keep being vigilant, we'll do whatever we can—as we are now—but it's certainly still a small but important, worrisome, part of my life. We can get better at avoiding it, at backing it off, but end of the day, it's a part of our life in this unique, remarkable family. Get used to it, make your own relationship to it, until you can strike your own peace with it. If you can do that, you and Lisa, are going to have unexpected, sometimes difficult moments, as you live wonderfully, exceptionally well."

"Mom, you're great, and that helps. And the idea that we're all working together on this is very good—at least, it gives me a more positive way to think about it." Lew raised both hands. "But we're not done, we're not where I'd like to be… Not even close."

"We'll keep working on this, on each and every specific part as they come up," Cash promised, "but you need to understand, and come to accept, that we can't get as far as you, as far as all of us, would like. It's what Callie said, 'you strike your own peace with it, and you go on to live wonderfully, exceptionally well.'"

"OK, I hear that…" Lew looked at each of the three of them, then said, "But I'm sorry guys, we need more… we need to do better. Lisa and I are going to have to think about this very carefully together. We need to figure out a way to be genuinely out of this… not worry about it so much… I'm sure we'll talk with Sara and Alvaro… when, if, we come up with some ideas that might work, we'll talk with you about them… Truthfully, that's the best I can do… I'm sorry…"

The Macher put his arm around Lew.

CHAPTER SIX

Stanley was on his boat, The Sunseeker 120 Yacht, that he'd playfully, uncharacteristically, renamed *The Hideaway*. Four days had gone by since he closed the real estate deal. It was three days since he'd finalized the truce and sent the letter to Cash. He took several days more than he'd planned, but all had gone well. He'd received the final payment four days ago, right after he'd returned the signed memorandum agreement for the real estate deal, and the following day, all $75,000,000 had been safely moved within the Panama account to his private high security numbered account. He'd been able to delay the filing of the paperwork for the real estate deal until yesterday. They had now been at sea for two days, and he was confirming with Alberto that all of the follow up details had proceeded as planned.

Stanley told Alberto. "I heard with Carl Stone, who signed off on your work. He was positive about it, especially the memorandum of agreement, which he agreed was final and unchangeable. He also approved of the letter to Cash and his people about the cease fire."

Alberto replied, "I appreciate that. In other good news, the buyers are pleased with the real estate deal. Also, Cash and his team seemed to be holding up their end of the cease fire. He has no idea that you've left, but he'll be reporting to Erik today."

"Good, I'll want you to listen in and monitor that meeting with both of them, then after you sign off, I'll talk with Erik."

"I'm already on the call, and I'll contact you after… I'll also report to Cash's designated monitor."

"Okay, fill me in on that as well."

"I will…I have a question. People will begin trying to reach you now that the required documents have been filed. What do I tell them?"

"To the extent that you can answer the questions, I'd prefer that. You can also email me questions through our secure system. I will answer your emails, though it may take several days. If necessary, and I mean only if it's absolutely necessary, you will be able to contact me via a code through our secure method. You can tell people that it may take several days before I respond. As you're aware, you will not know where I am or where I'm going. I'm giving you an important responsibility. Don't disappoint me."

"You can rely on me, sir."

"For your sake, I hope so." Stanley disconnected.

****

Erik and Cash had their first check in at 1:30 p.m. PT. Stanley, and all his crew, were with him, on the yacht, at sea, though Cash had no idea about their whereabouts. Cash, Callie, the Macher and Andre, were all in Seattle, in the kitchen at the restaurant. Cash went out the back kitchen door then upstairs to their apartment to have privacy for their call. On the yacht, Erik had gone below to be alone in his room downstairs. So far, the truce was working, and everyone was doing their part.

At 1:30 p.m. PT, as planned, Alberto initiated the conference call. There was a number for Erik and Cash to call in, which would allow the three of them to talk together.

Cash began, "So far, we're observing the agreed upon cease fire. Our entire team is either here in Seattle or on the way back from overseas. No one is investigating your principal's business activity. I sent photos to both of you this morning of all of us, here in Seattle, at the Pike Place Market."

"Yes, that was helpful," Erik replied. "We, too, have observed our truce. I sent photos of Ruben and Castro, Tim, and Johan with me at breakfast this morning. We're no longer tracking or observing you and your friends. I believe Alberto can confirm that."

"Yes, I saw a photo of them arriving in San Francisco, and I've confirmed with Stanley that they are working with him on a new project. Erik, can you specify this project?"

"Yes, they're working with Tim and I, researching new properties to acquire in California."

"Please send photos to me," Alberto asked.

"No problem," Erik said, then to Cash, "Any questions or concerns about the cease fire so far?"

"Alberto, I'd like you to confirm to Detective Samter that all is well."

"I will."

"Once you talk to Samter, I'm okay with the cease fire," Cash answered. "Do you have any questions or concerns for me?" he then asked.

"Only an update on your police captain, Jim Holden, in Miami, and your General Lopez."

"As you know, we can't control what they do, and we didn't promise to do that in our agreement. So long as you understand that, I can inform you that as a courtesy I told Captain Holden about our agreement and reassured him that neither Carlos nor Ruben would be in his jurisdiction. He was pleased to hear that and asked me to keep him informed."

"And the General?"

"I also told him about our truce. I also explained to him that I couldn't continue with the investigation, couldn't continue working with him or even be in Florida. I asked him to please back off, as a courtesy to me. He agreed to that, in the short term, and I asked him to talk with Alberto, our monitor. I'm sure that Alberto can confirm that. Beyond that, truthfully, without me and my team, he won't be able to learn much more about the real estate."

Alberto nodded. "I did talk with General Lopez, and what Cash is reporting is accurate. He's in Miami, standing down for the immediate future. He agreed to talk with me once a week."

"Let's revisit that in our next call. We'll have to put him off more forcefully, indefinitely."

Cash replied, "I didn't sign up for that, and I don't think I can make that happen."

"So long as he's on his own, in the short term, it's not a problem. Let me think about it, talk with my principal, and we may come back to you, Alberto, with some suggestions."

"I'll help however I can," Alberto replied.

"In that case," Erik said, "I'm satisfied with this call. We can regroup next week."

"I agree," Cash replied. "I appreciate everyone's good faith effort… Good-bye." Cash hung up.

****

Cash came back down from the apartment and into the kitchen, where his people were sitting around the maple prep table drinking fresh coffee or espresso and eating hot from-the-oven pastries that Callie had offered. They stopped talking when Cash came in, then waited for him to make a cappuccino and help himself to a warm strawberry tarte.

"Well?" Andre asked.

"As good as it could be. Everyone seems to be observing the cease fire. They did ask about General Lopez and Captain Jim Holden in Miami. I was able to reassure them that I'd spoken with both of them and for the moment, they were standing down. They're still worried about the General, and they're going to make some suggestions to Alberto. Alberto is also going to confirm to Ed Samter that all is well, then we'll talk about it again next week. My guess is that they're going to get Alberto to lead the General on a wild goose chase. I'm not sure how to deal with that. One other concern that I don't know what to do about. I have no idea where Stanley and his crew are. I wouldn't be surprised to find that they're off on another large yacht on their way to Mexico. Apparently, he hasn't told anyone where they're going. I asked Alberto privately and he doesn't know. I believe him. I'm not sure that it matters for us, except in the unlikely circumstance that we need to find him."

"That's consistent with his secretive nature," Andre observed. "He's always changing his name, his appearance, his location…"

The Macher's phone rang. He looked at who was calling then said, "I have to take this. It's the woman who's helping the General do research on the real estate." Itzac answered the phone and just listened. His expression changed, serious, uncharacteristic for him. "You're absolutely sure about this? You checked it twice… Can you get more specifics about the deal? Please try and call me back. And please don't tell anyone else about it yet…" The Macher squinted, looked around the table. "The situation has changed dramatically. They've already sold all of the real estate!"

"What? All of the Real Estate? Is that even possible?" Callie asked.

"Yes, apparently." The Macher replied.

"Is she one hundred percent reliable?" Cash asked.

"Absolutely. She was checking the Collier County Clerk records. The files came in late yesterday. The deal is done. All of the properties were sold to the Russell Group. She's trying to get more specifics. She's going to call me back."

Cash groaned. "Agh! Damnit! Agh...Stanley's so damn smart, and he moves like lightning… That son-of-a-bitch fooled us all, totally scammed us…and now, he's ahead of us again."

Andre couldn't help himself, "Hey, boss. Why do you think this keeps happening to you?"

Everyone, even Callie, had to laugh.

Cash shook his head. "Has to be because I hang out with a one-legged, dumb as dirt, miscreant… Kidding aside, we have to get on this right away. Let's regroup in an hour. I'll call the General. Itzac, can you try to find someone in the Russell Group that we can talk to?"

"Yeah, it's a big real estate outfit. I can reach out to the high-powered real estate people I know and try to get to someone."

Callie asked, "This changes everything, doesn't it?"

Cash nodded. "Yes, though I'm not sure yet, just what it means for us."

The Macher suggested, "Let's have this conversation later today—with the General. With any luck, by then, our researcher will have some more specifics, and I will have talked with someone with the Russell group."

****

Cash called the General right away. He reached him easily. "Mario, bad news," he said right away. "Stanley sold all of the real estate. All of it. The deal is already done."

"...damnit... are you sure?" The General asked, taken aback.

"Yes, it's been confirmed by your researcher, Nancy Lee, and she wouldn't tell the Macher that the deal was done if she wasn't sure."

"That changes everything."

"Yes, we all agree on that, but we don't yet know what it means. We're all meeting at the apartment in an hour. Can you call in then?"

"I wouldn't miss it. Call you soon."

****

At the meeting, the Macher started right in. "I made some headway. First, Nancy, our researcher, found some of the specifics of the deal in the Collier County Clerk Records. She went to the Collier County Clerk's website which allows you to search official records like deeds of sales. With the sales record she couldn't find a dollar amount, but she did find the parcel numbers. She then went to the Collier County Property Appraiser's website and entered the parcel numbers. That system includes real estate sales—which includes bare land, developed land, whatever property that gets bought or sold, or gets appraised for tax purposes. So far, she identified the total value of sales to the Russell Group as four hundred and twenty-five million dollars. She wasn't able to learn, though, the size of each payment or exactly where the money was sent. My real estate guy, Sammy Weiss, however, knows the man at the Russell Group who helped put the deal together. They're old friends, and he owes Sammy a favor. Sammy asked him if he could tell him where they sent the money, and the specific initial amounts. The Russell Group guy was impressed that he even knew the total, four hundred and twenty-five million. He told him, off the record, that they were told to wire the initial payments to Banco General in Panama. He said that they initially put up seventy-five million in two equal payments, thirty-seven million five hundred thousand each, over about a week. Over ten years total payments will come to four hundred and twenty-five million. That was recorded to the county. If it ever comes up, he wants the story to be that we got it from a connection with Collier County, which is mostly true. He said legally, the Russell Group must disclose it, but he doesn't want it to come from him."

"OK, it's a start," Cash said. "What do we know about the Banco General in Panama?"

The Macher nodded. "From my own experience, I know it's like the bank in the Cayman Islands, maximum security, high safety credentials, absolute confidentiality and so on."

The General spoke up, "I know that bank, we did some military transactions through them. I worked with them, several years ago. I think we should go there, today—right away—and try to freeze the account, before Stanley moves it again."

"You're as fast as Stanley," Cash observed. "Can we get a person in that bank to talk with us?"

"I'll call Sammy, see if he can get the account manager that the buyer was dealing with. We can start there," the Macher suggested.

"I can get the person that we dealt with for the military transactions," General Lopez volunteered. "Our transactions were big enough that he was pretty high up. We worked together several times, and he and I got along. I'm sure he'll meet with us."

"Will you make the same kind of argument that worked with the Cayman Island bank?" Cash asked.

"Yes, that's my plan, and I think it worked before not only because it's such a large and compelling case, but because the consequences to the bank of not freezing the assets pending an investigation, could be so dire. I know our guy there will bring in a compliance officer. He'll have to weigh the same calculation. The consequences of getting it wrong are hard to ignore. I'm going to ask my Venezuelan friend, Colonel Bolivar, to join us. He can speak for the military court. He's participated in several military court martials. On top of everything else, he's more aggressive, even meaner, than I am. I'll call him now."

Cash suggested, "Would you like the Macher to come meet you in Panama? I think I should stay clear of this, but the Macher can at least fly in his plane to be in Panama. He could be there if you needed to talk to him, or if you wanted him to check something out. Though I could argue that Stanley has violated our truce, it's not a direct violation. We never specified that he couldn't sell his property, so, for the moment, all of my people should stay clear of playing an active, identifiable role."

"Yes, I agree that the Macher should stay clear of the meeting, but he would be welcome to help out in whatever capacity he's comfortable. It would be especially helpful, if he could learn more about how the deal came together, how much money is finally involved, when it comes in, so on and so forth."

The Macher answered, "I already know how much is involved, and I can learn more about how the deal came together and the specifics. I'll call you later for all of those things. If you change your mind and want me in Panama, just know that though I intend to follow Cash's direction, I don't have Cash's concern about Stanley's wrath, both because I believe that Stanley broke the deal, and, don't forget, Stanley kidnapped Cash's wife's child, and he's now capable of hurting his daughter, Sara, or his wife. So, Cash does need to be very careful."

Callie touched the Macher's shoulder, appreciative.

"Thanks for explaining that. I understand," the General said. "Still, I think it might be prudent for you, Itzac, to stay back. As much as I value your help, I won't need you to make our case. It is, after all, money stolen from the Venezuelan military. Finally, I don't want to give Stanley an excuse to focus on you, Cash, Callie, Sara and so on."

"If you change your mind, we'll manage that..." Cash said, then changing gears, "OK then, I'm certain that Alberto made this deal for Stanley. He'll know who to talk to in the bank. I think, however, we should keep him out of it for now unless we want it to get back to Stanley."

"Keep him out of it. Absolutely," General Lopez insisted. "Our entire strategy depends on getting to the bank before Stanley tries to move his money again. That's why I want to go today."

The Macher spoke up, "Let's make our respective calls and plan to talk when you're at the airport."

"Good," the General said. "I'll make an appointment with the bank officer I know for late this afternoon, tomorrow morning, latest. I'll have him include a higher up compliance officer. I'll have Colonel Bolivar meet me in Panama."

"I'll have Sammy get us the name of the bank officer who managed the deal," the Macher added. "You can include him as well."

"That would be helpful," the General replied. "Thank you."

"Call us if there's anything else you need us to do from here," Cash said. "We'll stay by the phone."

"Good luck to you, General," Callie offered, as he went toward the door.

Before the General said his goodbyes, Andre offered, respectfully, "General, I think you and the Colonel will do wonderfully well... especially with the truly, remarkable windfall you just had—never underestimate your recent, unexpected stroke of luck, your unusual good fortune."

The General spoke up, on the speaker phone, confused, "Windfall? Stroke of luck? What are you talking about?"

Andre nodded. "My friend, you may not understand this yet, but you received a rare gift, a signal from God—it's like the miracle of Hanukkah—Cash is staying behind."

****

The General's contact at the Banco General in Panama was both extremely able and, like so many others who knew him, a loyal admirer of General Mario Lopez. At 1:00 p.m. Panama time, they were in a conference room at a round table with Jose Abrego, the General's friend, Romaldo Moreno, the manager of the Russell Group and Stanley's deal, and two compliance officers – Gabriela Perez, a tall middle-aged woman, and Manuel Cortez, an older senior compliance officer. Next to the General, charismatic in his military uniform, sat Colonel Daniel Bolivar, a tall, solid, very intimidating man also in a Venezuelan military uniform.

After Jose introduced the general, General Lopez articulately, forcefully, described the theft, including the amount of $350,000,000; the history, going back to the event over five years ago; the series of discoveries including the timing of the real estate deals, the role of Alberto, the lawyer who had experience moving money discretely from Venezuela and put this deal together, then managed the real estate; the series of murders: first Luis, a reporter who was already suspicious and actively researching this; then Garcia, who took an unauthorized photo of Stanley, and finally Rafael, a local police officer working on this. He detailed how Sara was badly beaten while Stanley's men were searching for the photo, how Alvaro was kidnapped, and he described the burning and bombing of Alvaro's club, then Alvaro's and Sara's home. Next, he told how Lew was kidnapped, then he described identifying Erik, Stanley's right-hand man, as a former Venezuelan military man working for General Gabriel, the man who originally stole the money before he died. Finally, he explained the elaborate secrecy concealing the investors in the real estate, how it was impossible to track the origins of the money, and so on.

When General Lopez was finished, Colonel Bolivar spoke about the ongoing investigation in Venezuela, and how the military investigators would like to subpoena Stanley and his cohorts in front of a military court martial. He went far enough to say that they thought the real estate was bought with stolen money and that the recent sale of the real estate was making the money more difficult to recover. Freezing the $75,000,000 in the numbered account of their bank would give them time to conclude their investigation, and, if they were right, enable them to renegotiate with the buyer to receive the money from the sale.

No one said a word for almost an hour while the General and the Colonel spoke. When they were finished, the bank officials asked specific questions for another hour, then they asked the General and the Colonel to leave the room to give them time to talk among themselves and consult others.

An hour and a half hour later, close to 4:30 p.m. local time, the General and the Colonel were called back into the room. Manuel Cortez spoke for the bank, "We have decided to freeze the account pending your investigation. We'll expect regular weekly reports from you, and we'll revisit this decision whenever we deem it necessary. We are obligated to tell the holders of the account immediately of our decision. We will be notifying them after this meeting. Thank you for bringing this to our attention, General Lopez. Our history with you made this an easier decision."

"Thank you for your prompt, helpful response," General Lopez replied. "We will keep you informed regularly." He got up as did Colonel Bolivar, and they went around the table personally shaking hands and thanking each of the Panamanians. General Lopez embraced his friend, Jose Abrego.

In the car, the General called Cash, "The account has been frozen," he announced. "The discussion was to the point, thorough and well handled. They're letting Stanley, or his representatives, know now as we speak. To use your movie language, "It's time to circle the wagons."

"Yes, that's already underway. You, too, need to arrange for safety measures."

"The Colonel has requested elite Venezuelan soldiers, men I also know, to guard us. Four of them will arrive tomorrow morning."

"Is there anything else we should know now?"

"I don't think so. We'll talk more tomorrow morning after we're back—let's say nine a.m. Seattle time, noon Miami time."

"Good, travel safely, and for now, congratulations—this is a job well done."

"Congratulations all around—to you, the Macher, even Andre for all of your work, and a special thank you to Colonel Bolivar, who's here with me. He did an exceptional job describing the investigation and the importance of freezing the account for the Venezuelans."

"Yes, thank you Colonel Bolivar, you've done an enormous service to all of us."

CHAPTER SEVEN

General Lopez and Colonel Bolivar were having a celebratory dinner at the airport, waiting for their plane, when Alberto got Stanley's call. It was 6:00 p.m. Miami time / 6:00 p.m. Panama time. It was 3:00 p.m. on Stanley's boat, which was traveling north along the Oregon Coast, almost to Washington, three days from San Francisco.

"This damn well better be important," Stanley angrily hissed at Alberto. "You know I told you I don't want to hear from you, ever, unless it's vitally important.'

"Please sit down," Alberto said. "I'm sorry to make this call, but this is vitally important."

"No more foolish talk, why are you calling?"

"I heard from the Banco General in Panama. They've frozen your account, pending an investigation."

"Is this a foolish joke?" Then softer still, "Are you out of control?"

"No, I just heard and its final. All seventy-five million is frozen. You can't move a penny out."

Stanley screamed. "That's impossible!"

"From what I was able to learn from Romaldo, our manager at the bank, Venezuelan military men made the case. He wouldn't reveal names, but I'm certain General Mario Lopez was their leader. Remember that he went and presented the case to the Cayman Island bank."

"You fucking idiot! How could you possibly let this happen? Don't answer that, there is no possible answer… Unless you can reverse this, right away, I will hold you responsible, you incompetent, miserable half-wit!"

Alberto made a coughing noise, then winced on the phone. "I'm sorry, but there was no way I could have anticipated this. And sir, I can't possibly reverse it. The General Banco of Panama is afraid of being embroiled in an international incident."

"There are no excuses!"

"Of course not… I understand."

"How could he know this so fast? I was going to move that money today or tomorrow."

"As you know, we had to file paperwork in the Collier County Clerk. As we discussed we delayed it until yesterday afternoon when the deal was absolutely unalterable. They must have had someone checking it this morning."

"Do you know the address where the General's staying in Miami?"

"Yes, he's at a hotel in South Beach. I'll send the address right away."

"It's apparently the only damn thing you can do… Now, I need to make a plan. In the meantime, if you hope to even imagine a future, you'll find a way to reverse this. Call them again, you miserable low-life reprobate… I'll call you later."

****

Stanley had everyone except Johan, who was piloting the yacht, gather in the aft deck. He didn't waste a minute, "We're stopping at Astoria, it's a port city in the northwest corner of Oregon, just across the Colombia River to Washington. Erik, I want you to arrange for our preferred private jet and Chris, the pilot we trust, to be waiting for us in Astoria. Ruben and Carlos, Erik will drive you to the small airport in Astoria. You should be able to meet Chris at 6:30 p.m. I want you to take the private jet from Astoria to Miami. Keep the jet waiting. Abduct the General from his South Beach hotel, the Beacon, tonight, whatever it takes. Here's the address…" He handed Ruben a piece of paper. "Next, take him back on the plane to Port Angeles on the Strait of Juan de Fuca; Drug him, sedate him, whatever works to bring him back alive. We'll be waiting for you in Port Angeles—it's only about nine hours from Astoria—where we'll make him our prisoner on the yacht."

****

General Mario Lopez and General Bolivar arrived at their South Beach hotel at 10:00 p.m. ET. In the lobby, they agreed to meet for breakfast at 10:00 a.m. to review their meeting before calling Cash and his people, then they said goodnight in the lobby. Colonel Bolivar went out, to meet an old Venezuelan retired military friend, also a colonel. He'd invited General Lopez, who also knew the colonel, to join them, but General Lopez apologized, excused himself, and went up to his room. The General was exhausted. He hung up his uniform, went to the bar where he'd added his own favorite rum, made a stiff drink, then sat in a comfortable armchair to enjoy it. He'd chosen a rum made in Venezuela—Diplomatico Reserva Exclusiva, distilled in copper pot stills and aged for twelve years. This rum is considered the best rum from Venezuela. He savored it, feeling good, then he went right to sleep.

At 5:00 a.m., Ruben and Carlos softly, ably, unlocked the front door of the General's room. The General was sleeping deeply, in bed, when Ruben injected a shot of Etorphine in his neck, a synthetic opioid, used to tranquilize large animals—the same knockout drug that the General had used on him not long ago. Before the General passed out, Ruben whispered, "Payback," and while Carlos held him down, Ruben, wearing gloves, vigorously poured a bag of fresh dog excrement over General Lopez's face and forcefully emptied a large portion of the dog's moist stool into his mouth. General Lopez woke up just barely—sluggishly, disoriented—then, as he passed out, he spewed the dog feces from his mouth onto Ruben's shirt and pants beside him. Before he was unconscious, Ruben, who was annoyed, urinated all over General Lopez's dog shit covered face.

****

At 8:30 a.m. PT, Cash, drinking coffee in Callie's kitchen, took a call from Colonel Bolivar. The colonel explained, "Mario and I made a date to have breakfast at 10:00 a.m. Miami time this morning. We were planning on reviewing our meeting before we called you. The General, who is always very punctual, didn't show up. I finally got the manager to meet me at his door. I could tell right away that someone had picked the lock and broken in. Inside, I could see that he was gone. I'm guessing that he was taken from his bed against his will."

"I'd bet he was kidnapped. He told me you were getting military guards this morning. Apparently, Stanley was ahead of us, again. Can you call me in half an hour? I'll have our entire team there at Callie's restaurant in the kitchen. We need to get him back, right away."

"I'll call in half an hour."

****

Cash called the Macher, then Andre, who was staying with a new young woman. They both agreed to come to the restaurant right away.

Callie, who was also in the kitchen now, had been listening in on the calls. She turned to Cash, "If you're right, and he's got the General on a boat, we need to get more help… Let's call Detective Samter, ask him to recruit his coast guard friends."

"Good idea, especially if he's headed south toward Mexico."

"My other idea is less obvious, but worth trying, especially if he's going north," Callie said, pensive.

"Canada?"

"Maybe, maybe Alaska."

"Yes, I know where you're going, and you're way ahead of me." Cash stood, put his arms around her from behind. "When did you get to be so smart?"

Callie turned, put her hands around Cash's neck. "I learned from this odd, difficult, character…good looking though." She turned, kissed him gently, then stepped back. "So, smarty pants?"

"If we're looking north, Corey Logan, has to be…"

"You never disappoint, babe. Call her, she should be in on this right away. Have her bring Abe, too, before this is over, we'll need him…"

"I'm afraid you're right about that, too… One more thing, please keep Sara out of this. We're doing again exactly what we worked so hard with her to avoid. I'm worried that she'll be upset."

"Babe, I understand why you're worried, but truthfully, I believe that you can rely on your daughter. End of the day, General Mario Lopez is a genuine friend, like family—she'll get that, and she'll do whatever she can to help him…"

"I hope you're right. Still, the last time around, she was ready to leave our family, it was that important for her to protect her own new family. So, if you're wrong, the stakes are very high."

"Yes, they are. I get that, but I'll bet you anything you want that Sara will be all in, unequivocally. Remember how mad she was when we didn't tell her right away about Alvaro… She's smart, and in every way that matters, she's your daughter."

"I so hope that you're right."

"I am right…"

In the midst of this horrible, frightening moment, when they feared for their new, dear friend's life, when they knew that they'd be risking their carefully constructed plan for Cash and Sara, for their entire extended family's well-being, they exchanged tender loving glances, looks that came from living complicated, self-aware, truly shared, lives.

****

At 9:30 a.m., the entire crew in Seattle were sitting together around Callie's comfortable long, maple prep kitchen table. From the prep table they had a view that sloped over the alley and down the hill to the waterfront below. Cash, Callie, Andre, the Macher, Detective Samter, Abe and Corey all sat quietly around the table drinking Callie's coffee. Colonel Bolivar was waiting on the speaker phone. The tone was somber, even gloomy, they were all worried about General Mario Lopez. Cash began by saying, "I had a call from Erik, Stanley's righthand man. He was blunt, there was no pretense about a cease fire or a truce. He wouldn't discuss what happened to the General, nor take any responsibility for it.

He did say in no uncertain terms that the General's well-being depended on our ability to convince the Banco General in Panama to cancel the freeze of Stanley's assets. There was no ambiguity about that. This was his message to us, period. I told him that I'd get back to him later today. My opinion is that we need to tell them that we'll try. They'll surely want us to show them how we're going to do that. Whatever we do, we need to buy time to keep the General safe, and to find out where they are."

The Macher spoke up, "Are we thinking that they're on a boat?"

"Yes, that seems to be Stanley's fallback position. I called Alberto as soon as Erik hung up. I told him that Stanley had kidnapped the General, so that his situation had changed dramatically. I explained that Colonel Bolivar was going to see him this morning, and that if he didn't help us right away, the Colonel would put him on a military plane back to Venezuela today to face a court martial. I scared him. I'm guessing Stanley has threatened him as well. Long story short, he was eager to help me. He said that Stanley and his men were on a yacht. When I asked for the specifics, he got the invoice and a brochure he'd received when he helped Stanley buy the new boat. The Sunseeker 120 Yacht, that he'd bought, and playfully, uncharacteristically, renamed *The Hideaway*, is 120' long, three years old, and cruises comfortably at twenty-two knots. He'll have a photo from the brochure, and the actual brochure for the Colonel when he arrives."

"Colonel Bolivar, will you go out to see him this morning, in his office? After I introduce you, can you apply your considerable persuasive powers to confirm all of those things? And see if you can find out any further info, anything at all, that might be helpful."

"No problem. I think that when he's reminded of the consequences of stealing money, hiding it, then kidnapping a former General, and of my ability to deliver those consequences, he'll be inclined to be helpful. Also, FYI, the four elite soldiers that the General and I requested from Venezuela have arrived. I'll leave one of them watching Alberto today, until I learn everything he knows. They're all available for you as this plan progresses."

"Excellent. I think you should plan on traveling to the west coast tonight with all four of the soldiers. As soon as we find the yacht, we'll need to move quickly... Now, I'll call Alberto and set that up right away."

"Good," the Colonel replied.

Cash frowned. "I'm sorry to be so scattered," he went on, "but the most important thing, the thing that has to be done first, is a call that you and I should make together. And we should make it ASAP. Let's talk to the General's contact at the Panama bank. We need his help to buy some time. Colonel, can you set that up, get him on the phone and patch me in?"

"I'll find him, wherever he is, and call you with him in fifteen minutes."

"Perfect. I'll be waiting." Before Cash hung up, the Colonel was gone.

Cash turned back to the crew around the prep table. "We have a few minutes before he calls back. Two things we ought to can get started on while we're waiting. Detective Samter, can you talk with your Coast Guard friends, tell them that we're looking for a Sunseeker 120 Yacht? Ask them to look south, from San Francisco toward Mexico. It's a large attractive boat, 120 feet long, and should be possible to recognize. Colonel Bolivar will have Alberto send us a photo this afternoon. If anyone spots it, have them specify the location and contact you right away. They should not board the yacht, do not let them know that they're looking for them. Our goal now is simply to locate them."

"I'll make those calls now." Samter excused himself, left the kitchen table to make his calls in the more private living room.

Cash looked at Callie, "Will you please take the lead with Corey?"

Callie nodded, smiled at her friend. "Though we think it's likely that the yacht is on its way to Mexico, it's possible that he's going north, into Canada. It would not be out of character for him to choose the unexpected direction. I know how well you know that country around Vancouver Island, then north up the Inside Passage all the way to Alaska. Is there any way that you could put the word out to others using these waters to keep an eye open for this yacht?"

Corey nodded. "There's a well-connected community among independent fishermen and fisherwomen. We communicate regularly with fishing information, weather reports, concentration of fishermen and so on. I can put out the word to my friends and they in turn can reach out to others. Before we're done, there will be more than fifty small fishing boats—Purse Seiners, Gillnetters, Trawlers, Trollers and so on—looking for that yacht. I'll spread the word and the details right away."

"That would be great," Callie replied. "Any siting, even a day or two before, will give us a place to start. And as Cash told Detective Samter, we don't want them to know we're looking for them. At this point, all we need is a location."

"I'll let you or Cash know immediately if I hear anything. I'm going to step out now to start calling." Corey, too, left the kitchen.

Abe, who'd been quiet, asked a question, "The General is an important man. Will they risk hurting him?"

"So long as there's any hope that he can help them get their money back, I don't think they'll hurt him… at least not now. All the more reason that I'd like to deliver that hope today."

Cash's phone rang, it was Colonel Bolivar who said, "I have Jose Abrego on the line. He's the officer at the bank with the long history with, and a genuine respect for, General Lopez. I told him that the General had been kidnapped and that we needed his help. Nothing more. Cash, can you fill him in?"

"First off, Mr. Abrego, I want to express to you, emphatically, that we're all committed to getting the General back safely."

"As am I. He's a valued friend, a fine and generous man. I'll do whatever I can to help."

"Thank you. Here's what we know. Stanley, who you know of, had his men kidnap him from his Miami hotel. We believe they've got him on a yacht, that left San Francisco two or three days ago. We don't know where they are. We don't even know what direction they've taken. We need time, at least several days, to find the yacht, then another day, or more, to figure out how to free the General. The only way we can get that kind of time is if you talk with them and convince them that you'll consider undoing the freeze, make Stanley's money available for him. This won't work unless you're genuinely convincing."

"I can be very convincing to help General Lopez."

Colonel Bolivar spoke up, "It goes without saying, but I want you to know, absolutely, that there will still be support among the Venezuelan military to help you in any way possible to save the General."

"Though I never doubted that, it will be helpful for me when I talk with my colleagues that you made it so clearly."

"Do not hesitate to call me along the way if I can be of any assistance."

"Thank you."

"And thank you, sir, for your unequivocal support..." Cash added. "To go on, if our plan works, you never need to actually release the assets in the accounts, you just have to make them believe that you're working on it, that you'll be doing it as soon as the necessary required steps are done."

"I can easily tell them that we're reconsidering freezing the assets. We're waiting now for compliance to do the necessary steps to undo such an important decision. I can say that they're meeting tomorrow to formalize redoing it. And then I can find another day or two for the bank higher ups to agree to it."

"I'll set up that call to Erik, right away. Give me an hour. Do you want any of your colleagues on the call?"

"Yes, I'll include one of our senior compliance people, Manuel Cortez, and Romaldo Moreno, the manager of the Russell Group and Stanley's deal. I know they'll help us with this when they understand the circumstances and what we actually plan to do, where we hope to end up. In the meantime, I'll explain to them what happened to the General."

"Please keep us posted," the Colonel requested.

"Of course," Jose replied.

"Excellent, I'll call you in an hour with Erik on the line." Cash ended the call.

****

Twenty-five minutes later, Colonel Bolivar was in Alberto's office. The Colonel was standing tall, intimidating, in front of Alberto's desk. Alberto had the brochure of The Sunseeker 120 Yacht on his desk and Colonel Bolivar was reading it carefully. It cruised at twenty-two knots but could run as fast as twenty-eight knots. It could comfortably take up to ten guests and five crew. The interior was well designed, spacious, and luxurious throughout. The Colonel put down the brochure. "Where are they? Where is this boat?"

"I have no idea, none... They left San Francisco several days ago but their destination is a carefully guarded secret. I don't think that any of Stanley's men, excepting perhaps Erik, his righthand man, know where they're going."

"I'm going to say this one time. If you can't help us find the General, you're going to be on a military plane to Venezuela before sundown."

"Colonel, please, I'll do what I can, but Stanley is both very unhappy and extremely angry with me—he irrationally blames me for what you did—freezing his assets at the Panamanian bank. Furthermore, I've never been a person he confided in. I'm happy to tell you what I know as soon as I learn it, but I can't do more than that."

"Write this down—you have two hours, maximum, to do much more than that. I want the marina where he kept the yacht in San Francisco. I want you to go through your files and provide any further material that may be relevant about the boat, about Stanley. Where does he do repairs, where does he fuel the boat, where does he buy food supplies, where does he do his banking in California, who takes care of his California estate when he's gone on the yacht, who are his doctors, how can we reach them, anything and everything. Go through your files, even a seemingly insignificant thing may be helpful. Also, fax three copies of the brochure to Cash Logan. Right away!"

"I will… right away."

"Impress me Alberto, the stakes for you couldn't be higher, and so far, you're well on your way to a court martial."

Alberto had turned red, and he was sweating. "I'll do my best, sir."

"I'm going to leave a soldier here, close by, to keep an eye on you. If you even think about running away, he'll bring you to the airport. Call me in an hour with a report." Without another word, the Colonel let in the Venezuelan soldier, said a few words in Spanish, and then he was gone.

****

Cash connected Jose, Manuel and Romaldo to Erik, and then, surprisingly, Erik put Stanley on the phone. Jose Abrego began, "Gentlemen, we've decided to reconsider the status of your account. For several reasons, that aren't important for us to detail on this call, we've recommended unfreezing your account. It will take several days to unravel all of the compliance issues, but that's already underway. On another unrelated matter, it's essential that General Mario Lopez be released, in good health, at an agreed upon location, if this is accomplished. We understand that this is not your affair, but we're hoping that you can be helpful, through your connections, to communicate that this is important."

Erik replied, "We don't know anything about General Lopez. We may be inclined to learn more about him when the account is open. Not before."

Manuel said, "Our compliance group is meeting tomorrow to formalize redoing it. In several days, your account will be open."

"Once that is done, we will continue this conversation," Erik replied.

Stanley spoke up for the first time. "So, we're absolutely clear, there is one thing that I need you to understand. We can't possibly do anything about the general you mentioned. We have no idea of his whereabouts or about his wellbeing. However, if you successfully reopen the account, quickly, we will be helpful if we can."

"We understand that the missing General is not your affair. However, if you could even ask your contacts about him, that would be appreciated, sir," Romaldo replied.

"I will give you two more days to unfreeze the account. That's all."

Jose spoke up, "We can't guarantee that. We don't control the compliance reversal process."

"And we can't control what might happen to your General before you find him."

"Let's speak tomorrow after our compliance group meeting, then every day until this is successfully resolved," Jose suggested.

"I will not be talking to you again until the account is reopened. No later than three days. Goodbye." Stanley got off the phone.

"Erik, I'd like to call you tomorrow afternoon and report on the compliance meeting," Jose tried again, "Will you take that call?"

"Yes, tomorrow we can still talk… Until tomorrow." Erik signed off.

Jose spoke to his colleagues, "Okay we have two full days. I'll call Colonel Bolivar and Cash, then report back to you. Thank you all."

****

Cash had made copies of the photos of the yacht in the brochure, and he was handing photos to Samter. He'd given some to Corey earlier, and she'd already made additional copies of the photo to pass around to fishermen and fisherwomen who were helping her. Now, Corey and the detective were all back around the kitchen table. Samter was explaining, "My Coast Guard friends will help, but as you know, it's a long stretch of water to cover."

"We did some rough calculations. The general went missing this morning. That means that they put him on a plane from Miami sometime last night. If the yacht is heading south, toward Mexico, they should be somewhere in southern California. I'd guess that they picked up the General well north of Los Angeles. They had to set him down at an airport—Monterey, Luis Obispo, even Santa Barbara. That, at least, can limit the area you have to cover."

"Yes, and the photo will help," Detective Samter held it up. "It's a beautiful, quite distinctive boat. I'll get it out to my people right away."

Corey was actually looking at the brochure. She held up at least 40 copies of the photo of the yacht. "These photos will go out this afternoon. My contacts are spreading a very wide net. Even so, if they haven't crossed into British Colombia yet, we won't find them. Our fishing boats will be covering Vancouver Island, Cambell River, Port Hardy, then up the Inside Passage as far as Prince Rupert. It's July, prime time for commercial salmon season up the Inside Passage and into Southeast Alaska. It's a lot of water but we'll have fifty to seventy-five boats keeping an eye out for the yacht. I'll let you know as soon as I learn anything."

****

Stanley was on the aft deck, talking with Erik. The *Hideaway*, their Sunseeker 120 Yacht, was traveling up the Inside Passage. It was early evening, and they'd just passed Port Hardy, going north up Queen Charlotte Strait. "I'm uneasy," Stanley said to Erik, the only person he actually confided in.

"How so?"

"They're smart. They have considerable resources to find the General. We need to rethink our end game."

"What are you thinking?"

"Until we get our money back—and because they want to save the General's life, I do think we'll get it back, if only for a day—let's stop moving north. Let's hunker down up one of these obscure inlets in wild country where we can hide, lost up the Inside Passage."

"You're ahead of me, please tell me more about what you're thinking."

"The only danger to us now, is that they'll somehow find us before they return our money. They have no idea where we are, so if we hide out in a safe obscure space, if we don't keep moving, we'll be invisible. Once we get our money out of this bank, we can hide it in another bank, then take our time, go slowly, carefully, and rethink our plan."

"That makes sense. We can stay put for a while, regroup."

"Right. We also need to think about how we want to handle the General. But if we get a float plane, once we get our money, we can drop him off anywhere, well south of here, and then, when we're ready, we can move north and disappear. We can have Ruben or Carlos eliminate the General later."

"I like this strategy. I'll identify an inlet not far from us, out of Queen Charlotte Strait, where we can turn into tonight, then hunker down tomorrow morning."

"It must be remote, well hidden, unlikely to be noticed."

"No problem. Boats rarely go up these remote dead-end inlets. If we go far enough, and take a side channel, select a secluded spot, we'll be on our own."

****

It was a busy, uneventful evening and night. Coast Guard boats were patrolling from San Francisco, Monterey, and Los Angeles. None of them had reported any sitings of the yacht.

Corey had put out the word to her fishing friends, and former co-workers, many of them Canadians, and they in turn reached out to their colleagues and friends, fishing along the Canadian coast. Corey had started fishing summers on a seiner in Alaska or in Canada with her mother, when she was a teenager, then continuing on her own after her mother died. Her mother, as a child, had been a Canadian citizen. Later, when she married an American, she chose dual citizenship, which Corey was eligible for. Over twenty plus years of fishing, working on boats in Alaska and often in Canada, she'd become a well-liked co-worker, friendly with many men and women who fished regularly. When she put out the word that a valued friend had been kidnapped and his life was at stake, the response was instant and emphatic—these people respected Corey and wanted to help however they could. By that evening, she had more than fifty fishing boats, eyes open, as they fished and traveled—north on the eastern coast of Vancouver Island, some passing Nanaimo, others Cambell River or Port Hardy, and a group scattered fishing up the Inside Passage all the way to Banks Island.

There was no response until the following morning. One of the boats reported seeing a yacht of that description yesterday morning, going north past Campbell River. They hadn't noticed anything unusual about the boat and only remembered it looking at the photo Corey had sent last night. It was a start.

Two hours later, this morning, they got a second sighting. A fisherman reported seeing the yacht going toward Port Hardy, last evening around dusk. Okay, they had a location to begin their search. A half hour later, Corey showed Cash, Callie and the others, including Colonel Bolivar who'd arrived last evening with four no-nonsense soldiers, a map with a route marked going up the Charlotte Strait past Queens Sound. After showing it, she said, "I sent eight of my people who were close by, to scour that area. Hopefully, they can spot them, follow them discretely and get a location where they spent the night. I've also sent my best, most trusted, friends, the four I chose and discussed with phase two, to go directly to Port Hardy. They'll be close by, ready, whenever we find the yacht. As I said, I've explained to them, in some detail, what we'll need them to do for phase two. They're all prepared to take a risk to save a good man's life. They're reliable people, and they're capable, often formidable."

Cash turned to Colonel Bolivar, "Can you get your soldiers on a private plane to Port Hardy right away. That will be our base until we locate them. We'll get a float plane to meet you there, to rendezvous with the fishermen and fisherwomen, when they've located the yacht. With any luck, we can do that tonight."

The Colonel nodded. "We came here on our military plane. It's standing by and can take us right away to Port Hardy. Can one of you arrange a reliable float plane?"

"I'll take care of that," Detective Samter said. "I have someone who's worked for me often. He's smart, able, and discrete. Colonel, I'll tell him you're in charge."

"Corey, you'll be our point person," Cash said. "Please go up to Port Hardy with the Colonel." He turned to the Colonel, "how many people can you comfortably take on this flight?"

"I can take Corey, my four soldiers, and as many others as you designate."

"Why don't you take Corey, Detective Samter and me in this flight. Callie, Abe, and Andre you can go today in the Macher's plane." He turned to Itzac, who'd anticipated this.

"We'll be ready to leave in an hour. Anyone else, anything else, we should bring?"

Cash looked around the kitchen table, no one added anything. "Okay, let's gather in Port Hardy this afternoon. Itzac, can you and Abe find rooms for us to stay and a place to gather. This is a lot of people, but this is going to be a big operation. Once we find them, we'll have to surround them and take over the yacht. We'll talk about who's doing what when we get there. But for now, I'll want the Colonel, Corey, Andre and me in charge of the takeover. That's a lot of asses to sit on one stool, but I absolutely trust, all of them, and as you'll see, we'll need them all." He turned to Andre, "That's the finest group you've ever been included in. It's also the nicest thing I've ever said to you." He made a zipping motion across his lips. "So, try to keep your insatiable appetite to provoke trouble to yourself." He pointed at Andre before he could make a nasty comment. "Okay, let's go."

****

The evening before, Erik had guided Johan, the skipper of the yacht, to the southern side of Bramham Island. They'd spent some time looking at their charts and chosen Seymour Inlet, an extremely remote inlet in very wild country accessible beyond Bramham Island. Seymour Inlet, long and narrow, was ridged on both sides by rugged hills as it worked its way through the huge wilderness Great Bear Rainforest in British Columbia. One of the things that made it so isolated was that to enter, you had to navigate Nakwakto Rapids, one of the fastest navigable tidal currents in the world. Directions say, "Mariners are strongly advised to navigate Nakwakto Rapids only at slack water. At no other time is it possible to navigate this rapid safely." Johan and Erik checked the tides and decided the best time to safely cross the rapids would be at slack water, 6:49 a.m. tomorrow morning. They anchored the yacht at a secluded cove to wait for early morning.

At 5:00 a.m., they followed Schooner Channel, the southern channel, a strait on the east side of Bramham Island to the rapids. At just about 6:49 a.m., it was a cautious and safe crossing at slack water, and then they were on the Seymour Inlet stretching forty-three miles inland to the Seymour River Delta. The river has its own side inlets, narrow waterways and forms a maze of complex, narrow waterways and tidal pools and lagoons. As they explored, they saw one small tug towing a log boom, one small seldom used logging camp, an aluminum crew boat going to that camp, and a single small fishing boat, a seiner. There were no pleasure boats. More than halfway down the Seymour River, they chose a side inlet that went north for miles. They found a narrow, secluded cove, untouched wilderness, where they felt safe to anchor between a narrow, wooded island, and the wooded shore. Unless a boat came around the island, unlikely even in traveled water, they were hidden.

****

Abe and the Macher had found and rented three old cabins, part of a well-intentioned, but slowly failing motel, not far from the water in Port Hardy. There were eleven of them, counting the Colonel's soldiers, so nobody wanted to think about who would sleep where if they had to sleep. Excepting the soldiers, who were storing their gear and waiting in the float plane moored at a nearby dock, all seven of them gathered in one of the cabins, cabin twelve, where Corey and Detective Samter were working two phones. Corey hung up the phone and announced, "We're striking out, no one has seen them, not even a hint of them when they stop and ask at a marina, or a fuel station, or a place to buy supplies.

I've told them to inquire wherever they can in the area we identified. It's like the yacht disappeared. I asked everyone on our team, about 50 boats, to send out an urgent request to anyone they know who's been in the designated area, to fish, to explore for fishing spots, or just traveling. So far, there's been no response. I can bring in more boats, but if they've chosen to hide out up one of any of the inlets, it's a lost cause."

Samter spoke up, "Two things, I called off the Coast Guard patrolling south, but I have one thought. We have a float plane and he's a first-rate pilot. If we get even a direction, he can go up and down checking out these inlets."

Corey nodded. "Thank you, it's the best idea so far, but remember they're travelling up the Inside Passage. It they decide to hide out, there are virtually unlimited inlets, each of them with many side inlets. We need a starting point, just one sighting last night. Let's give it another hour, see if we get anything at all from our urgent message."

Andre, who'd been listening carefully, said, "Our last sighting was near here, Port Hardy, last evening, right?"

Corey nodded, yes.

"If they're as smart as we think they are, I believe they will go up one of these unlimited inlets to hide out… but I don't think they'd try to do that in the dark. What I'm thinking is if you limit your search to two or three hours from Port Hardy, and ask if anyone has seen this yacht anchored, near one of those inlets off the eastern coast of the Queen Charlotte Strait—and remember that's not the side a fisherperson would be checking closely if they supposed they're running straight north through the strait—I think it greatly increases your chance of a sighting. Someone may have passed it by, anchored in a quiet spot, waiting for dawn." Andre pointed at Corey's map, "Specify South Passage, Cape Caution, even Bramham Island, and see if it gets any kind of response."

Corey smiled wide. "That's so smart! I'll put out that word right away?"

Callie put her arm around Andre. "I'll never let Cash give you a hard time again. From this moment on, we'll make him treat you as the brilliant strategist that you are." Callie kissed his cheek.

Andre, feeling pretty good, raised his middle finger at Cash.

****

Stanley had gathered all his people on the aft deck. They were relaxing. The mood was light, they felt safe, and this was like an unexpected vacation. The mood changed when Erik brought General Mario Lopez onto the aft deck. The general wore a black hood over his head, fastened tightly around his neck. His hands were cuffed behind his back, and though he could walk slowly, his ankles were shackled. Stanley made a gesture, and the aft deck was cleared except for the General, Erik, Ruben and Stanley. Erik put the General in a chair.

Stanley spoke to him, standing above him, "We've given them until sunset tomorrow to release our money. If they don't, your life is over. I'm thinking this is a good time for you to deliver a message to your friend at the bank, Jose Abrego. I'd like you to tell him that you don't know the people who've kidnapped you. You've been well treated, but that will all end if our money isn't released tomorrow. It needs to be signed and delivered and available for us to move all of the money the following morning, that's the day after tomorrow. Today, we're going to send them an unmistakable message – we're going to amputate your right little finger. We'll send them a photo of your little finger after we amputate it. We'll explain to him that your severed finger is what they call in a fancy restaurant an 'amuse bouche'—a treat, a taste if you will, before you begin your meal.

I want you to impress upon him that at 6:30 p.m. tomorrow evening, if we haven't received the required signed documents, we will amputate all of your other right fingers, four more. At 7:30 p.m., if we still haven't received the signed documents—which they can scan and email to us through our protected channel—and the signed directions to release the money in the morning, we will amputate all five of your left fingers.

If we have received the signed documents and the documents to move our money out of the bank, which we will return immediately with directions about where to send it when the bank opens. If all of that goes well, and the money is moved to our designated bank, we will return you by float plane to Seattle or there abouts, perfectly fine, excepting a missing little finger, a lasting memory of our encounter.

If, however, the money isn't received by our designated sender by 5:00 p.m. the day after tomorrow, more of your appendages—fingers, toes, ears, then entire hands and feet, and so on—will be amputated."

Stanley signaled Ruben, who picked the General out of the chair, stood him next to a counter. Next, he uncuffed his right wrist, re-cuffing the left wrist to a rail under the countertop. He raised his right wrist to the counter-top, signaled Erik to hold his wrist down with two hands. Ruben separated the General's fourth right finger from his right little finger. Holding them apart, he expertly severed the General's right little finger with a stainless steel Miltex amputation knife. The General screamed as the blood spread onto the counter. Ruben took several pictures before Erik covered the wound with a moist towel, then added thick gauze on his hand over his missing finger, organizing a make shift bandage under the towel.

"This is just the beginning," Stanley said. "Do you understand?"

The General responded, breathing with difficulty. "Yes...I will talk to Abrego...now."

****

Cash, Callie, Andre, the Macher, Abe, Ed Samter and Corey were all waiting in cabin twelve for some kind of report from the fishermen and fisherwomen. It's been over an hour, and they were worried. The phone rang, but it was Jose Abrego for Cash. "I'm putting you on the speaker," Cash said, as he set it up so everyone could hear.

"I had a call from the General," he explained. "He was bound and I'm guessing that he was blindfolded or hooded somehow, though I couldn't see him, because he said he couldn't see the others in the room.

Right before the call I got a photo texted to me. In the photo, a man's little finger had just been amputated. There was blood still gushing. The severed finger was lying in the blood, included in the photo. I was told it was General Lopez's finger in the photo."

"Damnit." Cash swore. "How was he when he called?"

"He was in pain, but coherent… He began by insisting that he didn't know who his kidnappers where. Furthermore, he said that except for his severed finger, he hadn't been hurt seriously. They had told him that there was a deadline to unfreeze Stanley's money by tomorrow at sunset, say seven p.m. Furthermore, they expected to be able to move the money, all of it, the following morning. They expect us to send signed documents unfreezing the money, then specific authorization to move it to wherever they specify the following morning. If all of that is accomplished, timely, they say they will release the General from a floatplane somewhere near Seattle, with no further harm. However, if it isn't done timely, they will begin amputating more of his appendages. The severed little finger was an example, an 'amuse bouche' they described it. Then they detailed further amputations, each one more severe than the last, unless all of their requests are accomplished timely. I think they mean it."

Cash answered, "I'm sure they mean it… I want you to meet their demands, timely, all of them. If we can locate them in time, we can save the General. We're in British Columbia trying to do that know. It's not impossible, but even if we find them, we may not be able to do that before you have to release the money. Because his life is certainly at stake, you have to be willing to move the money by their timeline, even if we haven't found them yet."

"I understand. You can rely on us."

"Thank you. We'll have to keep in close touch. We need to hope, we need to pray, that we can find them tonight or tomorrow, latest."

"Godspeed," Abrego said, then he signed off.

Cash looked around the table, the group looked anxious, troubled.

The Macher spoke up, "You said the right thing. We're doing what we have to do," then he expressed everyone's unspoken fear, "I only hope we can save the General's life; however this goes."

"I'm worried about that," Callie said, softly. "Even if we do everything they ask."

"I agree." Ed Samter, nodded. "His life is hanging by a thread."

Abe looked around, sensing the depressed tone, hoping to shift their mood. "In my work, you learn that if you're doing everything you can, doing it well, there are often unexpected opportunities that appear just when you think you've lost. You're a very impressive group and you have every reason to hope for success. I, for one, believe that you'll succeed."

It was quiet, a little more hopeful, as others considered that.

Then the phone rang again. Corey picked it up listened carefully, said to the phone please wait, put the caller on hold, stood up and yelled, "Yes. Yes! We got a sighting." She went back to the phone, went over everything again as she wrote down the details, then thanked the fisherwoman who'd called. She turned to the others, smiling wide, explaining, "Last night, the yacht was anchored on the south side of Bramham Island. That means that they're going up Seymour Inlet, and they were waiting for the slack tide to navigate across Nakwakto Rapids. They chose Schooner Channel, the southern channel, a strait on the east side of Bramham Island. I know that water and I can get us all through the rapids then up Seymour Inlet."

"That's what we needed," Cash said, "The four fishing boats that you've chosen for phase two should be sent to the south side of Bramham Island. Corey, you should specify exactly where and when we will meet them."

"No problem. Let's get the timing for the next slack tide that we can make with enough light to reach them."

Andre spoke up, "I have it, it's seven thirty-six a.m. tomorrow morning."

Corey said, "I'll set it up so we'll meet the fishing boats at six a.m. at the east side, at the end of Schooner Channel close to the rapids. I can specify that. That should give us time to get to the rapids before slack water."

Cash added, "We should go to the float plane about five a.m. The plane will have to make at least two trips. Trip one, will drop Corey at the end of Schooner Channel to get on one of the fishing boats to lead the crossing."

Corey went on, "That works. The first float plane should then drop the Colonel and the four soldiers so they can wait on land on Seymour Inlet on the shore. After the crossing, the fishing boats will pick them up there. The second trip will carry Andre, Cash and others to join the appropriate boats. One of us, I recommend Samter, should stay with the float plane, armed."

Samter nodded.

Cash added, "Callie and Itzac, will you stay behind, to coordinate with Samter and Corey via cell phone, and then importantly, prepare for the crucial phase after the capture. Abe, please pitch in whenever you can."

Abe responded, "I'll help as we go, however I can."

The Macher nodded. "Thanks, Abe, I'll call on you… I'll start with getting our prisoners discretely to the airport then secretly onto the Colonel's plane. Next, as soon as our captives are on their way to Venezuela with the Colonel on his military plane, I'll think through how all of the rest of us can get well away from Port Hardy, and get back home."

Callie added, "I already have an idea for the yacht."

Andre spoke up, loudly, "No, I'm absolutely not sneaking a multi-million-dollar yacht back across the border."

Callie smiled. "Sorry. You're taking charge of losing the boat. It's a done deal. You can sink it, or blow it up before the border, and avoid a crossing."

Everyone around the cabin said, "Yes, perfect."

Andre shook his head, not responding.

Cash went on, "Good. Now, let's have Samter, the colonel, Corey and I go up Seymour Inlet with the float plane tonight, at dusk. Let's see if we can spot the yacht from a discrete distant, without attracting attention."

"How are you going to examine a remote wilderness inlet with a float plane without attracting attention?" Callie asked.

Colonel Bolivar replied, "I have high powered night vision binoculars. You can see one thousand six hundred and forty feet with them day or night. Let's fly over the inlet, after dusk, after they're asleep."

Samter nodded, "Wildguarder Owler1 night vision goggles designed for hunting, right?"

"Exactly, but I use them regularly, day or night, for reconnaissance. They're excellent."

"I use them, too, and I have them with me. Let's go talk this over with Bill, our pilot," Samter said.

****

At the seaplane, Bill, the pilot, was explaining, "I can fly over the inlet, in the dark, but there could be noise." Bill checked the weather, "we've got some rain coming in after dark, that should help."

"Let's do it late then, say after midnight," the Colonel offered. "They should be asleep. And the rain will camouflage the noise."

"It's risky, most seaplanes don't fly at night, but up here, we can do it, so long as we don't need to land in the water before we're back. We'll stay as high as we can, so at night they won't see us. It's dangerous, though, so let's limit our passengers."

Cash suggested, "Let's include the Colonel, so he can use his night vision binoculars. And Corey, because she'll know where to look."

Cash turned to Samter, "Ed, can Corey use your night vision binoculars?"

"Yes, of course."

"Can we confidently rely on these night vision binoculars at midnight in the rain?" Cash asked.

"Yes, definitely," the Colonel replied.

Samter nodded agreement.

"OK…" Bill's tone had changed, it was more grim. "I've got to ask… Detective Samter, this could go badly…are you sure you're okay with it?"

"I've been thinking about that, and yes, as sure as I could be. We need to save a good man's life. If we can find the yacht and turn the fishing boats loose early with clear directions about where to go, this could work. Under no circumstances, however, can the people on the yacht know that we're searching for them."

"I can't guarantee that," Bill explained. "But after midnight, flying high, with the rain, it's unlikely."

"OK then, suppose we meet here at eleven p.m., see what we can find," Corey suggested.

"That's good," Bill responded.

"Thank you, Bill," Samter spoke for all of them. "This is above and beyond what you have to do, and we're very grateful."

****

Stanley and his crew were on the aft deck, after finishing a late dinner. They were drinking cognac, that Stanley had stored on board, and feeling relaxed. Erik came in from below with an announcement.

"We got an email, sent through our system, from Jose Abrego, at the Banco General in Panama. Basically, they've agreed to send the documents that release the freeze tomorrow morning. They're also sending specific authorization to move the money, wherever we specify, the following morning… They did say that they'd be holding back fifty percent of the money until they receive the General alive and well." He'd printed the email, and he passed it around.

Stanley read it carefully, then again. "Excepting the holdback, it's what we asked, when we wanted it… Let's send them back an email saying that the holdback, even 10%, is unacceptable. Reiterate that we're not holding the General, that we didn't kidnap him. Tell them that if they hold back any of our money, the kidnapper will likely torture the General…"

"I understand… Truthfully, even if they add a wrinkle, I think, one way or another, they'll pay all of the money… They've decided to save the General's life, at any cost," Erik added, "and they'd like to avoid a more serious follow up then our 'amuse bouche.'"

"Let's find out, right away." Stanley had dictated the email, and he passed it on to Erik. Stanley turned to the others, "Ruben, Carlos, what do you think we should do with the General?"

"Once we get the money, let's kill him, bury him at sea. If we let him go, he'll come back to hurt us. He'll keep trying to find a way to get the money, and he isn't stupid."

Erik asked, "If we kill him, won't we have many more Venezuelan military types looking for us?"

"They've been looking for us for years, and as Ruben said, if we let him live, he'll still come after us… If we disappear, as Stanley has said we would, let them look. They have no idea where we are, no idea where we're going. No one but Stanley and Erik know that… New identities in a new, unexpected place is our future." Carlos said.

Stanley nodded. "Yes, and more on that later, but first I'd like to weigh in on the General. I concur with Ruben and Carlos, I think he'll never stop, and we need to eliminate him. However, my sense of timing is slightly different. To get all of our money back right away, which is our primary goal, we may need to send him back, a free man. I think we can do that, to Seattle, simultaneously with receiving all of our money. But there is no reason that we can't eliminate him in Seattle, days later. Erik & Carlos, I suspect that you would both enjoy that."

Ruben smiled. "I still have a score to settle with Callie James in Seattle. Nothing would please me more than to eliminate her and the General simultaneously, colorfully, in Seattle. Do we have time in our plans to allow for that?"

"Yes, I think so. But first, it's time you all knew more specifically about our plans," Stanley said. "By now, you've probably guessed that we're going first to Alaska. What you don't know is that I already own an estate outside of Anchorage with a large home where we can comfortably hide out. This is, however, just a safe hideout. From there I intend to retire to a vineyard. Either in France, or, if possible, back to our vineyard in California. We'll have to change our identities again. This time, I've chosen another Spanish speaking nationality, Argentina, a country where people are known as experienced wine growers… This choice is obviously up to each of you. But if you choose to do it, you can rest assured that it's reliable. Erik has been managing that."

People around the table nodded, Ruben added, "Yes, especially after the General dies, that would be good."

Stanley went on, "You'll all be welcome at the vineyard, but you may choose to move on to other things. You can also choose another new identity with a different nationality. That's entirely up to you. You will have plenty of time in Alaska to think about other choices, and, of course, take a trip back to Seattle to settle old scores."

Tim, who rarely volunteered an opinion, spoke up, "I, for one, think it's a good time to end this chapter, to start again. Bravo Stanley, you've proven, yet again, that you're truly gifted, a cat with nine lives."

CHAPTER EIGHT

Corey, the Colonel and Bill, the pilot, were flying over Seymour Inlet. It was after midnight, cloudy, raining steadily, with regular gusts of wind. They'd covered about half of the inlet, staying between 800–1100 feet high as they crossed the inlet exploring all of the possible hiding places. They'd looked at all of the spots Corey knew, though she didn't know them by name—Charlotte Bay, Harriet Cove, Wawatle Bay, Frederick Bay, Schaffer Point and more. Their night vision binoculars worked well, and they were able to survey the areas they passed, but until now, though they'd seen an old, abandoned logging camp, they'd seen no boats at all. The rain was not a torrential storm, but rather a steady downfall, giving them some cover. It was almost 1:15 a.m. when they passed Safe Cove and reached Mansell Bay, a midsized inlet going north to their left.

For more than the first half of the inlet, there was nothing unusual to see. About two-thirds of the way up, there was a narrow, secluded cove, untouched wilderness, between a narrow, wooded island, and the wooded shore. From their position, high and away, Corey saw the yacht. Immediately, she cried out to Bill, "Move away, fast! Go to the far shore and back out of the inlet. They're right behind that island."

Bill swerved the float plane away from the island, going due south now, toward the Seymour River. The Colonel turned to Corey, "I saw it too. We're far enough away that they surely didn't see us. Someone would have to be wide awake, standing outside in the rain to have even heard the faintest sound at all."

Bill nodded. "We were lucky, and I think we're good. Let's go home."

Corey high fived Bill, then the Colonel, "Sometimes, things actually do work out. I know exactly where they are, and it won't be hard to bring the fishing boats to surround them in that little cove… Well done, gentleman."

****

At 7:00 a.m. Corey was on one of the fishing boats, at the east side of Bramham Island, at the end of Schooner Channel close to the rapids, preparing to lead the crossing at slack water at 7:36 a.m. The first float plane trip had already dropped the Colonel and four soldiers to wait on land beyond the crossing on an accessible shore on the river, Seymour Inlet, where the fishing boats would pick them up after their crossing.

The second float plane trip was already underway, carrying Andre and Cash to join the appropriate boats. Samter was staying with the float plane, armed. At 8:30 a.m., after an uneventful crossing, two of the fishing boats stopped again at an accessible point on shore to pick up either Andre or Cash. Corey was leading the fourth boat having comfortably taken charge of allocating people to their respectable boats. There was a soldier, an experienced sniper, strategically positioned, one on each four boats.

Corey led all four fishing boats to Mansell Bay. The float plane would join them there, after they'd surrounded the yacht.

****

Stanley, and some of his cohorts—Ruben, Carlos, Johan and Tim—were on the aft deck, enjoying coffee and pastries, a late morning snack. It was about 11:30 a.m. Erik came up with an email he'd printed out.

"We heard back from Jose Abrego, from the Banco General in Panama. They proposed a compromise, as you predicted. They'll send half the money tomorrow morning, the other half at the same time that the General steps off the float plane in Seattle in good condition… He specifies a place where they can see the General as they wire the rest of the money. It's a pier, in Elliot Bay, just on Queen Anne Hill. The

General gets off on the pier. Our man covers him, when you confirm the wire, our man lets him go. What do you think?"

"That will work. They will surely cancel the money if we don't free the General. I can accept this offer. We'll get all of our money, and we'll be long gone before we come back at him..." Stanley nodded, pleased. "It appears that we're going to get our money back tomorrow. Erik, get our pilot, Chris, on a float plane, to pick up the General tomorrow at noon and take him to Seattle with Carlos. After we get our money, our pilot will bring Carlos back to the yacht." Stanley was feeling good, uncharacteristically festive, glad that this was resolved. He pointed at Ruben. "I'd send you, Ruben, but since they fed you that disgusting dog shit cocktail, I'd be worried you'd lose control, kill the General in the last moment."

Ruben looked at Stanley, perfectly serious. "Truthfully, you're smart not to take that chance."

"I know," Stanley nodded, then he turned to Erik, "Let's respond to their email, tell them we agree, and let's get our pilot set to pick up Carlos and the General tomorrow. You and I can work out where."

"Will do." Erik went downstairs.

That's when Stanley spotted the first fishing boat, the one Corey was piloting, turn into their secluded cove. He signaled to Ruben and Carlos, who were bringing out high powered assault weapons. As they raised their assault rifles pointed at the first fishing boat, a second, then a third, and finally a fourth fishing boat surrounded the yacht in a semicircle, blocking their exit from the secluded hidden cove. In the boats, the fishermen and fisherwomen had taken cover. The snipers were in position, ready to fire, but hidden from sight.

Cash spoke into a bullhorn, "Stanley, this is Cash Logan. We're here to free General Lopez. Put down your weapons and no one will get hurt."

Stanley didn't respond. Instead, he turned, gave a signal, and Ruben and Carlos began firing, each one on a different boat.

Instantly, before they could do any real damage, one sniper killed Ruben and another one killed Carlos. They tumbled to the deck, each of them shot in the head. It happened so suddenly that people on deck, including Stanley, were stunned, shocked.

Cash spoke again, loudly, "Raise your hands, all of you, instantly, or more of you will die."

Stanley, Johan and Tim raised their hands.

Cash went on, "Several of our soldiers, and others, are going to board your boat, take you prisoner and free the General. You will be killed at the slightest effort or movement to escape." A sniper fired a shot over Stanley's head, a convincing warning.

One at a time, fishing boats came alongside the yacht. At the first boat, an armed sniper and the Colonel came on board, then a sniper and Cash, who'd been on the phone, came on board. The soldiers handcuffed Stanley, Johan and Tim. Next, with their hands cuffed behind their backs, another handcuff, behind each of them, was locked to the deck rail.

At this moment, the float plane landed behind the fishing boats. The float plane came alongside the yacht, and Detective Samter came aboard, armed. Next the third fishing boat came along side and an armed sniper and Andre came aboard the boat. Two of the snipers, Cash and the Colonel, had already gone down below to find the General.

****

With a worn, often used tool on his key chain, the Colonel unlocked the lock, opening the door to the lower-level bedroom where, they judged, the General was being held prisoner. They found him inside. General Mario Lopez had a black sack over his head, his wrists were tied tightly behind his back, and his ankles were securely tied to his chair. The casual bandage on his right little finger was noticeable. When Cash took the black sack off of his head, the General blinked repeatedly, having difficulty seeing in the light.

The Colonel untied his hands, then his feet.

Cash took a look at his poorly bandaged, missing little finger on his right hand. "We'll get this taken care of upstairs."

The General nodded.

Cash put a hand on his shoulder. "Mario, you can't imagine how glad I am to see you."

The General, who was breathing slowly, carefully, took Cash's hand, holding faintly, but as firmly as he could, with both of his own hands. "You're a lifesaver, Cash Logan, and you, too, Colonel Bolivar. A lifesaver!"

"You're free, and you're safe," Cash assured him.

"Did they hurt you, anything more than your missing finger?" The Colonel asked.

And before the General could answer, Cash added, "If you need it, we'll put you in the float plane and take you to the hospital."

The General took another careful breath, "No, I'm exhausted, dehydrated, very hungry, my missing finger hurts, and I'm still scared, but I wasn't seriously hurt after my finger."

"The 'seriously' worries me. Don't hesitate, anything at all?"

"Well, when they kidnapped me, I was tormented by their thug Ruben. He pasted dog excrement on my face then forced dog stool into my mouth. But that was the worst of it. It was payback for what Callie and Andre did to him. He knew I was there. They didn't inflict any real, lasting physical injuries beyond my finger."

"If it helps, Ruben's dead upstairs. One of the Colonel's snipers shot him in the head."

"Thank you," the General touched the Colonel's arm.

The General stood, slowly, then hesitantly stretched his arms and legs. "I need a minute before we go upstairs," he requested. "Then, after you clean up and rebandage my hand, I'd like to interrogate the boss, the guy who organized, then executed all that we've been investigating."

"That would be Stanley," Cash said.

"Okay, before I start in with him, can you please review what we know. Truthfully, I'm not thinking clearly yet, not really remembering details, and I'd like to be ready for him." The General sat on the bed, taking slow breaths, getting his bearings.

"Can your finger wait until I fill you in on this?"

"Yes, for a little while longer. Sadly, I'm used to it." He looked up at Cash, attentive.

Cash nodded. "OK. You know most of this, but let me summarize. Here's what we believe about Stanley. He invested the stolen money wisely, in lucrative real estate developments that he expanded into three substantial high-end properties, all of them in Florida, in and around Naples. Recently, as discretely as possible, he sold them all to the Russell Group, and had the first two payments deposited in the Banco General of Panama. As soon as we learned about that, you went to the bank. Stanley definitely kidnapped you right after that, after you froze his assets at the Panama Bank. So, you know, your friend at the bank, Jose Abrego, has been working with us nonstop to find you. He's just been great, and I'll fill you in on those details later. We suspect Stanley was aware of the theft, possibly early on, and we know that his role was to make three hundred and fifty million dollars of stolen money disappear. He did just that, expertly. There's one other wrinkle that we never figured out. Early on, someone took a photo of him in his lawyer's office. You've seen that photo."

"Yes, I remember when the Macher showed it to me. I had no idea who it was, nor did I see the significance of the photo."

"Stanley went to great lengths to get that photo back, including badly beating and mercilessly killing several people, some of them relatives or friends of ours. We never understood why it was so very important. Meeting him, you may be able to shed some light on this."

"I doubt it, but I'll try. Let's get started, you've got me ready to begin."

The Colonel went on, "Stanley's handcuffed upstairs. We can take you to him."

"Good, let's see if he'll talk."

Cash smiled, saying, "Something tells me that right about now, you'll be able to get him talking about everything."

The Colonel added, "I can't wait for that."

The General got up off of the bed. "Let's go and get started. God knows, it's long overdue."

Outside the bedroom, the soldiers reported that they'd searched all of the bedrooms and other rooms downstairs and no one else was there. The Colonel told them to bring down two more people, search the entire area once more, as thoroughly as possible. Cash nodded, confirming.

At the stairway, the General turned to Cash and the Colonel, "I'm eager to begin with Stanley, but please, let's keep this first session limited, just a start. Truthfully, I need to go where I can take a good shower, a good meal, a stiff drink and think about all of this—my good fortune. Having all of you rescue me makes me understand the importance, the immeasurable value of hope."

Cash nodded, smiling, as the Colonel helped the General upstairs.

****

Upstairs, on the aft deck, the captives all stood, still cuffed to the rail. One of the snipers still kept a rifle on the prisoners. Andre and Corey sat around the table. Samter and the third soldier had gone downstairs to help finish the search.

They brought the General first to the table where Andre and Corey greeted him enthusiastically, affectionately. Right away, Corey and Andre washed his hand thoroughly, then they applied strong antibiotics and rebuilt the bandage on his missing right little finger.

When they'd finished working on the General's new bandage, Cash and the Colonel had Stanley's handcuff to the rail released, then sat him on a chair, facing the table. When he saw the General, he turned away and looked down. It was too late. The general stood, stepped over to Stanley, roughly took his neck in his left hand, firmly, stood him up, took his covid mask off, looked him in the eyes for several seconds, then squeezed his neck, hard, shouting, "You miserable son of a bitch!" Then louder still, "You lowlife bastard!" With his left hand, he slapped Stanley in the face, then again, even though Stanley was handcuffed.

The General turned to the Colonel, who was also standing, took Stanley by the neck again. "Do you know who this pitiful, vile retch is? Do you recognize him?"

The Colonel shook his head, no.

Holding his head high, held tightly by his neck, General Mario Lopez announced, loudly, "This is a dead man, this is General Gabriel Castillo, the man who stole three hundred and fifty million dollars from the Venezuelan army over five years ago. This man died soon after the theft. He was proven dead, identified as dead, confirmed as dead by multiple sworn witnesses. Yet here he is. Yes, this is unquestionably General Gabriel Castillo, back from the dead, moving our stolen money, yet again!"

"They will be thrilled in Venezuela to get our money back, and as you American's say, the cherry on the ice-cream sundae will be discovering that the legendary General, Gabriel Castillo, is still alive," the Colonel announced, pleased.

After a beat, the General added, "Alive and facing the rest of his life in a Venezuelan prison."

The General turned to a soldier, ordering, "Unhandcuff his right hand, keep his left hand handcuffed to the back of the chair."

The soldier did exactly as he was told.

The General grabbed Gabriel Castillo's right wrist, then raised his right hand, pointed it at Cash. There was a small, but visible red-purple thickened scar on the back and right side of his hand snaking down from his fourth and little pinky finger. The General explained, "This is why he was desperate to get the photo. No one would recognize his face with the mask he was wearing, but a shrewd observer, one who knew what he was looking for, could have seen this unusual scar on the back and side of his right hand, and this small but unmistakable keloid scar could have identified him. I only know about it because when I knew him, before he disappeared, he tried to treat it, have it removed, unsuccessfully. Foolishly, after I saw his unrecognizable face, I didn't even think to look for it in the photo."

Cash nodded, "Of course, none of us even knew to look for a small scar."

The General took over, demonstrably feeling better, and quite naturally taking charge, "Colonel, could you please call your colleagues in Venezuela? Tell them who you're bringing home."

"My friend, it would be my pleasure… And I'll make sure that you get the credit you deserve."

"Thank you… Can your pilot fly the prisoner to Venezuela tonight?"

"Yes, absolutely. We'll have the Macher set it up to discretely put General Gabriel, me and two soldiers on the plane at the Port Hardy airport. The flight will leave tonight from Port Hardy to a military base our armed forces colleagues choose. We'll have a regular warm military welcome for him."

Stanley was quiet, unsettled.

****

General Lopez's interrogation of Stanley was postponed as they made their plans. The revelation of precisely who he was answered so many questions, and it made getting him to Venezuela a top priority. The military court martial would do the heavy lifting of interrogating General Gabriel Castillo for as long as it took to learn everything. They decided to put Stanley/General Castillo on the float plane with the Colonel and two soldiers to keep an eye on him at all times. They'd take the first group—General Castillo, the soldiers and the Colonel—on the Colonel's plane tonight, a red eye, right to a designated military base in Venezuela. The Colonel said, he'd request a second plane for Gabriel's people, the other soldiers and anyone else we decided to send. One call from Colonel Bolivar was all it took to set that up and set the expedited timing. This was clearly a big deal, and when the Colonel explained that General Lopez hoped to recover most of the money, the reaction could only be described as wild uproar, approaching pandemonium.

Eventually, after the excitement calmed down, the Colonel made certain that everyone listening understood that General Lopez was the principal Venezuelan responsible for finding Stanley, identifying him as General Cabrillo, and would be taking the lead in recovering the stolen money.

Though General Lopez wasn't on the call, afterword, he said to his friends still on the yacht that he felt a great burden had been taken off his back. He no longer had to worry that any adversary, or anyone else, would be able to accuse him of collaborating, in any way, with stealing the missing money. In its way, he said, it was a real turning point, an important victory for him personally. All of his friends listening—Cash, Andre, Ed Samter and Corey understood and though they weren't loud, their response was visibly genuine admiration, fondness and understanding.

****

General Lopez told them he was already thinking about structuring the deal with the Russell Group. While they were still considering that, Samter and the two other soldiers who'd been assigned to thoroughly search, then search again, every room of the yacht came back upstairs. Samter explained, "We went over every room, including closets, storage areas, everything, twice – there's no one else on this yacht."

Cash pointed out, "We're missing Erik, Stanley's righthand man."

Colonel Bolivar took over questioning on that with unexpected enthusiasm. Apparently, there was considerable residual anger at General Gabriel Castillo among Venezuelan military leaders. When the Colonel persisted, including threatening a sharp knife to his nose, Stanley a.k.a. Gabriel said, "After we took General Lopez, Erik took the same plane back to San Francisco, where he's supervising closing down our existing business activities." Even under pressure, Stanley couldn't provide meaningful contact information for Erik. He insisted that their arrangement was that he and Erik would contact via secure email. He said he was willing to provide that information, but under the circumstances, which Erik was certainly able to discover, no one believed that Erik would respond. Cash intervened before Colonel

Bolivar actually hurt General Castillo. He said simply, "Let's move on. We don't need Erik. Colonel, you can revisit this more forcefully in Venezuela."

Corey took charge of releasing the fishing boats. She gave them the timing for the next reachable slack water and specific suggestions for crossing the rapids. Before they left, she wrote a check to each captain for $3,000. The General, Cash, and the Macher, by phone, had all agreed to chip in. They also promised to send each captain a case of their preferred whiskey. That was the General's suggestion, and Corey happily organized it.

Next, they put General Castillo, two able soldiers, and the Colonel on the float plane. The General was still handcuffed, then securely tied down to his seat on the plane. He sat between two armed soldiers. Those staying on the yacht conveyed fond farewells to the Colonel before he went onto the plane. Cash and the General were particularly effusive. They all said goodbye and thanked Bill, the pilot. They'd already arranged with the Macher to have a van to discretely take the General to the Colonel's plane at the small Port Hardy airport. Those on the yacht all waved goodbye as the float plane took off smartly from the water. It was a punctuation mark, an ending of a long, difficult period of battling fiercely with Stanley, now General Gabriel Castillo, then smartly, aggressively pursuing and capturing the Hideaway, his Sunseeker 120 Yacht.

It was agreed that Andre and Corey would pilot the Sunseeker 120 Yacht, carrying the rest of the crew and the remaining prisoners, back to Port Hardy. The remaining prisoners were handcuffed downstairs, in an empty bedroom, which was then locked. They, at least, would be out of sight until the yacht got back to Port Hardy.

Andre had agreed to take the yacht from Port Hardy. Earlier, he was told to make it disappear, leave it in a lonely place, submerged, or better yet, blow it up into unrecognizable debris, flotsam and jetsam, but no one believed he'd ever do either of those things.

Before they left, they discussed what to do with Ruben's and Carlos' bodies. Andre had already located very heavy weights in a gym area on the yacht to attach securely to each body. The voters decided unanimously to sink them in the heavy water, at least a mile apart, in the main channel of Seymour Inlet. Samter abstained.

****

The trip back on the Sunseeker 120 Yacht was actually relaxing after all of the stress of finding and then capturing Stanley a.k.a. General Gabriel Castillo's yacht. Now, Cash and Samter were sitting at the table, enjoying a beer. The General was lying back, nearby, on a lounge chair. He turned to Cash and Samter. "Do any of you know the person at the Russell Group who made this deal?"

Cash spoke up, "Call the Macher, he spoke with someone connected to them."

General Lopez called the Macher, who picked right up. Right away, the General asked if he'd had any dealings with the Russell Group.

"Yes, I can help you with that," the Macher replied, "My friend, Sammy Weiss, has talked with the man in charge of making the deal. I see where you're going General. I'll have Sammy set up a meeting with you and this man, right away."

"Thank you Itzac. I'd like you and your man Sammy to be at that meeting."

"My pleasure. Am I right in assuming that the Russell Group is going to keep the real estate, and they're going to respect the deal that they made, except that they'll transfer the payment to a group you designate controlled by the Venezuelan military?"

"That's what I've been working on."

"Can you tell me more?"

"You're pretty close already, Itzac, with a couple, as yet, unnegotiated wrinkles. Most importantly, the timing of the balance of the money will be sped up. Seventy-five million has already been paid. The balance of three hundred and fifty million, or a total of four hundred and twenty-five million, as the deal requires, will be paid over five years, maximum, rather than ten years. And as you can guess, there are other specifics, such as the interest rate, and so on, that will be adjusted. I'd bet it's a very short negotiation."

The Macher laughed, adding, "I'd bet it's the shortest negotiation in the history of the Russell Group. You'll tell the Russell Group that they simply have two choices: Remake the nature of the deal with the money going to the Venezuelan government as you just specified or face a variety of international criminal charges for buying illegitimate property, paid by money stolen from the Venezuelan military. That's shorthand, but it's something like that?"

"Itzac, I always loved how smart you are."

"Thank you. You're a gentleman."

"The key word is 'where I designate,' since I'm modifying one important thing—I don't want all of the money going to the Venezuelan military. As you know, I don't support the existing Maduro government. I, in fact, am planning to direct a significant part of the money to excellent human rights organizations, places that focus on correcting human rights abuses by the Maduro government."

"They'll be furious about that."

"If I set it up properly, the Russell Group will be satisfied they're in the clear, and no one will ever know precisely how much money I recovered, nor exactly where the money is going. I'll need your help. If we do that as only we can do it, the Venezuelans will never know about it, and if anyone even suspects it, they won't be able to do anything about it."

"I'll be happy to help with that. You're a good man, General. Well done."

****

Cash, Samter and General Lopez were enjoying the lovely ride in the spacious yacht. Before they reached the rapids, Corey anchored near shore to give them about half an hour to wait for slack water. Once the slack water was there, Corey expertly took the yacht through the rapids, and soon they were moving more quickly, crossing the Queen Charlotte Strait toward Port Hardy.

At a lull, Samter, curious, asked Cash, "What ever happened to Alberto, Stanley's lawyer?"

"It's a good question. Last time I talked to him, he knew that Stanley was furious. Rightly or wrongly, Stanley believed that Alberto contributed to his problems with the Banco Generale of Panama. Apparently, Alberto suggested the manager, Romaldo, at the bank who was handling his account, and Alberto filed the sale in the Collier County clerk before Stanley could move the money—that allowed us to know what he'd done. Basically, Stanley believed that Alberto was managing this and should have been prepared when we moved so quickly. Alberto was only doing what he had to do, but it was too late. He'd unwittingly triggered General Lopez into immediate, enraged action."

The General nodded, "Until that happened, we didn't really know what to do. We certainly had no idea who Stanley was or understood what he was capable of."

"Stanley was right, Alberto wasn't ready. He didn't anticipate what we did, and I think afterward, Alberto feared for his life. Long story short, I'd bet that Alberto is long gone, drinking mojitos on some forgotten Caribbean beach."

"Should we try to find him, put him in jail?" Samter asked.

"I don't think so. He's paid a high price—his business, his home, his way of life—and end of the day, he wasn't a decision maker. He wasn't even part of the substantive conversations. He certainly didn't know about, or participate in, the violence that Ruben and Carlos carried out for Stanley."

"Do you think he knew who he was working for?"

"Never. All he ever communicated to me was that Stanley never wanted to see him in person. He explained that most importantly, Stanley's goal was to be invisible, literally unseen."

The General offered, "He was invisible for at least five years. Truthfully, in his way, Stanley was a genius."

Cash nodded. "I'd never say or admit that, but it's true. He managed to disappear, totally avoided the Venezuelan military over five years, created a real estate empire with hundreds of millions of dollars with stolen money, apparently even financed a thriving vineyard. He lived a private, secretive lifestyle in luxury, without ever attracting attention, without ever meeting anyone."

"Didn't he meet Alberto?"

"The only time he met him was when the photo of him was taken and then because of that, Stanley got angry with Alberto and started hurting, even killing people. In doing that, he inadvertently brought us into his dangerous world, then little by little, things came undone."

"I think his mistake was to hurt your daughter."

"You're a true friend, but you've given me too much credit. Yes, that certainly got us all involved, but it was you, General Lopez—" Cash pointed to the General, a sort of tip of the hat, a *chapeau*. "—who drove the stake into his heart."

The General responded sincerely, "Now, you're giving me too much credit. Truthfully, we were a formidable team, all of us, I don't think Stanley/General Cabrillo ever understood who he'd unleashed."

****

It was almost 9:30 p.m. when Corey and Andre brought the lavish Hideaway, Sunseeker 120 Yacht alongside the dock near the cabins on Port Hardy. Abe, Callie and the Macher were waiting there and tied the yacht to the dock as Cash, Samter, the General, then Corey and Andre walked onto the dock.

As Callie and Abe led them to the tables they'd set up for an charcoal grilled outdoor dinner, the two remaining soldiers took the two handcuffed captives to cabin eight, which Abe and the Macher had set it up to hold them until their plane came.

Not surprisingly, Callie had prepared a lovely dinner, as only she could do it, for everyone else. She had two charcoal grills going outside in front of cabin twelve. Old plates from the cabins were set on two tables they'd attached together. The Macher had inexplicably found, then set up, a combination of flame lit outdoor oil lamps and tabletop torches on each table so that there was more than enough light to see dinner and each other.

With Abe's help, Callie brought out ribeye steaks, corn on the cob—buttered then seasoned with garlic and onion powder before wrapped in aluminum foil—sliced mushrooms and onions seasoned with red wine vinegar, olive oil, soy sauce and garlic, marinated in an open aluminum foil in a high-sided basket, prepared coleslaw with her own special sauce, and freshly cooked warm French fries set aside in a closed container. There was wine and whiskey, as well as ice, open on both tables and everyone helped themselves to large drinks, mostly Glenmorangie single malt scotch, as they sat together around the comfortably well-lit tables.

Abe, Callie and the Macher where especially pleased to finally see the General alive and well. They'd each worried, privately, that they'd never see him again. After a quiet, heartfelt moment, Callie raised a glass, "Mario, General Lopez, I'd like to propose a toast. I think I can speak for all of us that being here with you is a special moment… We're a very close, very private, unconventional, extended family. It's a loving group that has been together through many difficult situations—fierce adversaries, life threatening, unexpected hardships with dear friends and family member's lives at stake. It's a hard group to be part of, harder still to be accepted or included into. When you were kidnapped, when we feared for your life, all of us realized how you, in your low key, singular way, had become an important part of our extended family. Without drawing attention to yourself, you gently worked your way into our hearts… We're thrilled that you're safe. We're proud, we're lucky, to call you a true friend… Mario Lopez, we love you so very much."

Glasses clicked in tribute. Their faces expressed genuine admiration, then spontaneously, cheers rose all around.

After a festive interlude, General Mario Lopez, raised a large glass of scotch. He looked around purposely, making eye contact with each and every one of them, then offered, "I can't tell you all how happy, how grateful, I'm feeling being with all of you tonight. I wasn't sure I'd ever see you again, but because of you, my extraordinary friends, I never lost hope. Early on, after they captured me, I started thinking about you. I actually came to understand something significant, after all of you rescued me… I saw the importance, the enormous value of hope.

The Macher asked, "I do know an expression that's relevant. May I add a little something?"

"Of course."

"The expression is "Hope Dies Last." That expression came from a woman, a retired farm worker, she was recounting the days before Cesar Chavez and his stoop-labor colleagues founded the United Farm Workers… Studs Terkel, a wonderful writer, immortalized the farm worker, de la Cruz's, words in his book Hope Dies Last: Keeping the Faith in Difficult Times... I think it's what we, here, in our small extended family, work to do together."

"Yes, you helped me understand that… Hope Dies Last… I never lost hope because of you, my dear new friends… Truthfully, you saved my life."

EPILOGUE

(3 months later)

Callie and Cash were celebrating their second anniversary. They'd been married on the beach, just below Abe and Corey's cabin overlooking a remote wild hard to reach stretch of the Inside Passage. The cabin sat on a pear-shaped island near the Fiordland Recreation Area, a 225,000-acre mountainous wilderness of islands, inlets, fiords, waterfalls, rivers and glaciers. Callie asked him to marry her there on his fiftieth birthday, a surprise at a surprise party she'd organized. That meant that today, on their second anniversary, Cash had just turned fifty-two.

Tonight, Sara and Lew had insisted on hosting the party. To that end, they'd proposed a treat. First, they were having a drink at Callie's restaurant, upstairs near the bar, at their favorite table with Sara and Alvaro, Lew and his lovely girlfriend, Lisa. Lisa was now twenty-two, a year older than Lew, and they'd been together for more than four years. Cash and Callie thought they did wonderfully well together and especially liked how Lew had aged so gracefully into such a kind, thoughtful, young man living with her. They were both in college, at UC Berkeley, at the end of their sophomore year. They'd rented an apartment together as freshmen and since then, they'd been inseparable. Tonight, Lew wore an attractive grey suit that Lisa had picked out for him, and a tasteful blue tie with tiny white spots. Lisa wore a stunning long black dress. Clearly, it was a special occasion for them.

Sara also wore a black dress. Her dress was shorter, and she looked ready for Salsa dancing. Alvaro wore a black suit, and she and Sara made a beautiful couple. The four of them, Lew and Lisa, Sara and Alvaro, had become fast friends, and plainly enjoyed each other's company. Tonight, the six of them were meeting at 7:00 p.m. for a drink. After they were going out to Canlis, a favorite, classic Seattle restaurant. Dinner was at 8:30 p.m.

Sara and Lew had ordered champagne for the table, and Jill brought glasses and a bottle, explaining simply that it was the best champagne in the restaurant, and she'd been saving it for a special occasion. After she poured for all of them, she brought out, opened and set down a second bottle of the same champagne. Lew thanked her, charmingly, then raised his glass, taking charge.

He began, "This is a toast to my mother and my stepdad. To explain it, I have to go back to a conversation more than three months ago, when I described how hard it was for me to live in fear of being caught up in dangerous events, specifically being kidnapped, because of things that I didn't do, things that grew out of my stepdad and his friends high-powered conflicts… Since then, I thought about it a lot, and discussed it at length, first with Lisa and then with Sara and Alvaro… I digress now to toast the three of them." Lew clicked glasses with each of them, then said, "They are three of the finest, best friends a man could have. Sara has struggled with the same issue, and Alvaro, and Lisa, most of all, have insisted on working with me to find a realistic option that we can all live with."

He raised his glass again, "To two of my favorite people in the world, Sara and Alvaro." The six of them clicked glasses again.

Callie added, "I don't know where you're going, but I can unequivocally toast to that."

Cash joined in, "Absolutely true for me, too."

They all clicked again, took another sip, then Lew filled all of their glasses again. "And yet another toast to Lisa—my absolute role model, my standard of perfection, my unquestionably best friend and adored partner…"

Lisa kissed him passionately as everyone else cheered.

Callie raised a glass, "Lisa, you've helped my son become a fine young man. I love and admire both of you."

Cash added another toast, "To these two wonderful young people who are so captivating, so exciting to be with, and who have, together, grown into such fine young adults."

More glasses clicking, cheers and general good feeling all around.

Lew continued. "Let's finish this excellent champagne, then we have to go someplace else to continue our toast. Sara and I have taken the liberty of canceling our dinner reservation, and we rented a boat for the rest of our celebration."

"Totally unnecessary," Callie said, then smiling, "…but that's wonderful."

"You've outdone yourselves," Cash added.

"It's our pleasure. The boat is waiting for us at a dock on Elliot Bay." Lew turned to Sara. "Will you please take over to get us to the next phase?"

Sara nodded. "Absolutely." She smiled, as she began, "As we talked about this complicated issue, for all of us, the most important thing—unequivocally - was to stay close with, stay connected to, our wonderful eccentric family. Our goal was to find a way that didn't put us or our children in avoidable danger. The more we all talked about that the more we agreed that our last time on the boat together was very special, more than just a time to figure out next steps, it was a time to be close together without unnecessary fear or unwanted distractions… So that brings us to the boat we're about to see, and where we go from there."

Lew nodded. "Well put, a very nice introduction to what comes next. Now, let's go to the boat."

****

The limo was out front, and they brought their champagne into the back. The driver took them to the boat, waiting for them at a dock on Elliot Bay. Along the way, Sara explained that a few close friends would join them there. From there, the party would proceed out onto Puget Sound.

When the limo left them off on the dock, they walked toward the yacht from behind. Standing there waiting for them were the Macher and Andre.

Andre took the lead, and from a distant, they saw the aft deck first. It was spacious, beautifully designed and furnished with lovely woods and tasteful pieces. Callie went first and when she got closer, she cried out, thrilled with the boat's new name, The Bronze Pig, the English version of her restaurant, Le Cochon Bronze. Underneath she saw that a nickname had been added, "aka The Pig." She recognized the name of Andre's special cocktail that he used to serve, even though it irritated her, at her bar. She called Cash over, said to him, "Andre renamed this boat for tonight."

Cash nodded, laughing.

The Macher came onto the boat with Andre. They all sat around the table on the aft deck. Lew poured more champagne.

Cash turned to look around, "This attractive boat is somehow familiar. Sara or Lew, tell me, where did you rent it?"

The Macher pointed at Andre. "Tell them, Andre."

"I'll start at the end… The idea of this boat came from Lew and Sara. It's an anniversary gift from all of us, your friends. Callie and Cash, this is now your boat."

"Don't be silly. This is a very expensive boat."

Andre nodded. "This boat belonged to someone wanted by the police so I was able to make an unconventional arrangement. Most importantly, I received new ownership papers." Andre went on, "Look carefully. This boat's been totally redesigned, refurnished. All of this has been done, carefully crafted to suit your tastes."

Cash laughed. "Andre, oh my God, you stole this boat. This is Stanley/General Cabrillo's boat, the boat that you were supposed to sink or destroy."

The Macher tipped a hat at Andre. "Yes, he took a different tact. I helped out. I had a trusted friend, an accomplished international yacht dealer in another country, reinvent it's past, acquire it, legally—though I didn't want to know how—then sell it to me at a very reasonable rate. I, in turn, worked with Lew and Sara, and now, at Lew and Sara's suggestion, this boat, *The Pig*, is exclusively, legally, owned by Cash Logan and Callie James."

Lew raised his glass, "So this brings Sara and me to tell the rest of our toast. For Andre who doesn't know the history - this conversation began with a conversation more than three months ago, when I described how hard it was for me to live in fear of being caught up in dangerous events, specifically being kidnapped, because of things that I didn't do, things that grew out of my stepdad and his friends high-powered conflicts… Since then, I thought about it a lot, and discussed it at length, first with Lisa and then with Sara and Alvaro… Sara, had initiated similar conversations that led to our year on a boat, trying to figure out a way to eliminate those dangers. These plans worked in part, until Alvaro's cousin, Luis, asked him to hide a photo, and then all hell broke loose. So, we reviewed the thinking on the boat, and subsequent ideas. Long story short, with such interesting, uncommon parents and their eccentric friends, we simply couldn't find a way to eliminate risk and the possible ensuing danger. So, we were stuck, and we decided to start over." With a nod, Lew passed the story on to Sara.

Sara went on, "What we all agreed was that we had to live in separate places, away from our family and friends, places where we felt safer."

Callie and Cash shared an uneasy look.

"For Alvaro and our family, that's Cuba. Lew and Lisa were undecided. In the short term, it would have to be California, but later they were leaning toward further away—seriously considering Mexico, Spain or France. Lew even suggested learning Italian, then buying a house in Tuscany. But they haven't decided yet. Wherever it ends up being, it couldn't be anywhere close to our family." Sara passed the story back to Lew.

Cash and Callie were holding hands, plainly worried now.

Lew looked at his mom and stepdad. "Hang on folks…please stay with us." He went on, "Now, this is important, however distant, isolated or far away we were—and remember this—we still want to stay very close, connected with our family and their wonderful, unusual friends." He touched each of their shoulders. "That's when we took an unexpected turn. It occurred to us that we had this closeness and an acceptable level of safety when we spent a year on a boat. What if we had a fine boat, like this one, that was our safe house, a place where we could live on, disappear on, if necessary, if there was danger. We could live in separate relatively safe places, away from our family and their friends. But what if we gave our parents this boat, and committed to spend three to six months living on it with them together every year. We could include others to meet us at various ports and to improvise as we go. We want to keep trying, to be who we are, living separately in safe places. But we hope to live on the boat every year, for at least three months, maybe more. Let's see where it goes. We may do it even more often, but let's see it as an ongoing conversation, a way to both be with each other and look after one another. It won't be perfect, but it's a step forward."

The cheering was genuine and very enthusiastic, glasses were raised all around. Clicked, then clicked again.

Callie came over and kissed her son and then his girlfriend. Simultaneously, Cash embraced Sara and Alvaro.

The Macher added his own toast, "The young people have gotten ahead of their parents—Mazel Tov! L'chaim!"

Andre joined in, "To life." Andre pointed downstairs telling all of them, "Follow me, let's continue our celebration downstairs."

Sara, Lew, and their partners went below. Andre and the Macher led Cash and Callie down to the spacious downstairs gathering room. It was dark inside. When Cash and Callie were downstairs, the Macher turned on the lights. The large interior was filled with their good friends. Sara and Lew were in front singing Happy Anniversary. About thirty people stood, singing with them. They were all drinking and toasting champagne. Cash and Callie were speechless, seeing some of their very best friends all there beside them. They went around the room, crying out joyfully when they saw their old friends, many from past adventures, hugging and kissing each and every one of them. They included: Sgt. Lincoln & his wife, Cherry, from LA, Nestor and his wife, Lillana, Eva, Sara's Cuban doctor, from Cuba, General Lopez, Colonel Bolivar, Jose Abrego, Abe & Corey, Ed Samter and his fiancé, Kate, Mary, Callie's old friend - the doctor who'd confirmed that Cash and Sara where father and daughter, Will, Callie's maître d', Jill, the bartender, and Cesaire, her chef from the restaurant, and of course, Sara & Alvara, Lew & Lisa, The Macher, Andre, and so on.

After Callie and Cash visited comfortably with their friends, Sara and Lew whispered to one another, making a plan.

Then Sara began, "So let's set sail out on Puget Sound for the Pig's anniversary voyage. Some of our guests this evening will tell stories about your triumphs capturing wanted, criminal n'er-do-wells at sea, in this instance, from the Caribbean near Haiti then bringing them to Cuba, or just recently from the Inside Passage on Seymour Inlet all the way to Venezuela."

Lew continued, "And, of course, we'll feature Cash and Sara singing *Crazy*, Sara singing *Tonight is What it Means to be Young*, with the Macher accompanying them on the piano." Lew pointed the piano already set up in the corner. "And if we can convince her, Sara and Alvaro will present astonishing Salsa dancing.

Then, before the evening is over my friends, Cash and Callie will speak about themselves, about each other, about what they feel fortunate about having together. And we can all add things that they deserve to celebrate about on this occasion."

The Macher toasted, "Mazel Tov! L'chaim!"

Andre joined in, "To life."

General Mario Lopez, clicked his glass, then raised a toast, "To my dear friends, 'First, 'To Life.' Glasses clicked and then the General raised his glass yet again, "And then to share what these wonderful people taught me about the importance of hope... Because of them, I held on to it, I learned to rely on it, and that hope saved my life when I was kidnapped. And now, as I look around here,

I understand that Cash and Corey have put together this remarkable group of friends, of loved ones, because hope is part of who they are, their way of life, it's worked its way into their souls, and without doing it self-consciously, without even knowing it, they pass it on to love ones, to dear friends, to those of us here.

It's how their children, Sara and Lew, and their partners, can try such an unconventional living solution wanting to stay close with their family without putting themselves and their children in unnecessary danger. Based on their experience, they have reason to hope, to believe, that unconventional solutions can actually work. So those of you who are lucky enough to have it, to believe in hope—and as I look around this room, I'm sure that includes all of you—cherish it, protect it, and when you absolutely have to, rely on it… It will be there…"

AFTERWORD

(eighteen months later)

Cash and Callie were enjoying dinner at their favorite table, upstairs next to the corner of the bar in her restaurant. Cash's phone rang. He recognized General Lopez, calling him from his home in Buenos Aires. "Hello Mario?" He said.

"Cash, I hope you're well. Are you sitting down?" Mario asked.

"Yes, Callie and I are having dinner at our favorite table upstairs at the bar in her restaurant."

"Can you include her on this call?"

"Yes, of course. I'm putting this on the speaker." He did. They exchanged hellos. "Great to hear your voice, Mario. What's the occasion?" Cash asked.

"There's no nice way to tell this… General Gabriel Castillo escaped."

Callie and Cash yelled simultaneously. "Goddammit…" Cash roared.

"Pardon my French, but MERDE…" Callie added, "How is this possible?"

Mario sighed, then replied, "You remember just after your children gifted you the yacht, you reported that you'd found a secret compartment skillfully hidden down below. You supposed that that's where his friend Erik had hidden and later escaped."

"Yes, that's right."

"Well apparently, two days ago, someone landed a helicopter in the open inside outdoor enclosure area of the military prison. General Castillo, who was taking his regular walk in the area, simply stepped into the helicopter and then he was gone… It gets worse. I got a photo today, in express mail. It has Erik and General Castillo on a remote, unspecified beach, drinking cocktails."

"He's unstoppable!... What the hell can we do?" Callie asked.

Mario spoke softly, "I thought about that carefully before calling you… My conclusion—I think we do nothing… We got the money back… He's lost… He signed the back of the photo… Adieu!"

"He's saying goodbye," Callie said.

"You're right - it's a farewell." Cash laughed out loud, a rousing heartfelt laugh, then Callie started laughing loudly, too. Cash could see the tears pouring down her face. From Buenos Aires, a wonderful laugh joined in. The laughter was joyous, deeply felt.

When they were finished, happy tears of relief spilling all around, Callie finally spoke, "Mario, I'll expect you and your lovely wife for dinner, in Paris, tomorrow night, Au Pied de Cochon. It's a legendary restaurant in Les Halles, which was once the largest central wholesale food market in Paris. Les Halles flourished from the 12th century to 1973. In 1947, Au Pied de Cochon was the first resturant in Paris to remain open permanently three hundred and sixty-five days a year. The restaurant is still remarkable, a classic, open twenty-four hours a day, seven days a week. I'm confident that our entire family—Cash & I, Sara, Alvaro, Y.C, aka baby Cash, Lew, Lisa, The Macher, Andre, Corey, Abe and, of course, both of you, will be joining us.

Not long ago, you learned, hauntingly, that yes, hope dies last. Now, my dear, I hope to teach you a little known, oddly compatible insight—fine Classic French cuisine lasts forever."

Acknowledgements

Tyson Cornell, Jacob Epstein, Brendan Kiley, Ron Mardigian, John McCaffrey, Dorothy Escribano Weissbourd

www.ingramcontent.com/pod-product-compliance
Lightning Source LLC
Chambersburg PA
CBHW030743120726
47947CB00013B/5